THE NURSE

ABIGAIL REBEKAH

VOYAGER
- PRESS -

First published by Voyager Press 2025

Copyright © 2025 Abigail Rebekah

All rights reserved. No part of this publication may be reproduced, stored or transmitted in any form or by any means, electronic, mechanical, photocopying, recording, scanning, or otherwise without written permission from the publisher. It is illegal to copy this book, post it to a website, or distribute it by any other means without permission.

First Edition

ISBN: 978-1-0683212-0-7 (Paperback)

ISBN: 978-1-0683212-1-4 (Hardcover)

Original Cover Concept by Abigail Rebekah

Cover Design by Carlos Paulo César M.

Scripture quotations are from the Holy Bible, English Standard Version, copyright © 2001, 2007, 2011, 2016 by Crossway Bibles, a division of Good News Publishers. Used by permission.
All rights reserved.

Dear Sharny,
I hope you enjoy this!
  Abigail Rebekah
      xx

DEDICATION

This book is dedicated to the heroes of World War II.
"We will remember them."

CONTENTS

Chapter 1 ·· 1
Chapter 2 ·· 7
Chapter 3 ·· 13
Chapter 4 ·· 19
Chapter 5 ·· 23
Chapter 6 ·· 29
Chapter 7 ·· 33
Chapter 8 ·· 37
Chapter 9 ·· 41
Chapter 10 ·· 45
Chapter 11 ·· 49
Chapter 12 ·· 55
Chapter 13 ·· 59
Chapter 14 ·· 63
Chapter 15 ·· 65
Chapter 16 ·· 69
Chapter 17 ·· 73
Chapter 18 ·· 77
Chapter 19 ·· 81
Chapter 20 ·· 85

Chapter 21	89
Chapter 22	93
Chapter 23	101
Chapter 24	109
Chapter 25	115
Chapter 26	121
Chapter 27	129
Chapter 28	133
Chapter 29	141
Chapter 30	147
Chapter 31	153
Chapter 32	161
Acknowledgement	169

CHAPTER ONE

"Nearly there," the soldier whispered as he and another man ran through the mud, carrying the stretcher that held his best friend's broken body.

"Stay with us, Ed. You've got to," he pleaded.

The young man's bloodshot eyes flicked open; his pupils dilated. He lay restless, groaning deeply with every jolt of the stretcher. The sky blurred, spiralling like a tunnel, then the blackness came, and his body fell limp. Another jerk tugged him back into semi-consciousness as they slipped in the mud. He trembled all over, moaning slowly.

Drops of blood fell on the ground below as the two soldiers pushed uphill, towards the medic's tent. The sky above them was a haze of smoke and rain.

Explosions nearby sent tremors moaning beneath their feet. The cries of both wounded and dying men haunted the air.

Trees that once stood proudly above the soft green grass, boasting verdant foliage hanging gracefully from auburn limbs, now resembled charred stumps, destroyed by the raging fires and machines that kept flinging the land into shuddering fits.

Twisted wire burrowed deep into the ground; barbed hooks lay embedded in the uniforms of many soldiers as they lay there, unable to release themselves from the cruel entrapment.

"Denni, he's not going to make it," the other soldier shook his head sadly at the young man lying on the stretcher, ribbons of dried blood trickling down his pale face.

No...no, you mustn't...you're all I've got, Ed. Please...no! Denni screamed silently at his best friend as they ran on.

The soldier's coarse uniform was plastered with mud. The frayed cloth around his wound was stained by the crimson fluid oozing from his body.

As the soldiers neared the tent known as the "hospital" they could hear the soft reassuring tones of the nurses alongside the constant groans of the wounded.

"Please, we need help!" Denni beckoned to one of the nurses. She quickly led them inside and towards a makeshift bed situated near the end of the tent.

"Keep that pressure on the wound; I'll fetch some morphine," the nurse hesitated for a moment, then quickly walked away. Denni couldn't help but notice her hands trembling; but somehow despite the overwhelming stress this nurse was enduring, her face possessed a smile that was soothing to look at.

The two soldiers lifted Ed gently off the stretcher, and onto the bed. The red stain colouring his uniform grew darker by the minute, his lifeblood draining away despite the force of Denni's hand. Denni crouched down beside him, pleading with him to stay alive. As he implored his best friend, the nurse returned with the morphine.

"This will help relieve the pain," she said tenderly as she administered the drug and gently removed the blood-soaked clothing. Despite the horrific appearance of his wound, she never flinched or shied away. Denni watched her in silence as she clamped the pulsing artery, causing the bleeding to stop completely. *Her delicate fingers are so perfect for a task that required such precise movement,* he thought.

"He was awful brave out there. That's why he was hit," Denni muttered, trying to conceal the anguish he was feeling.

"You've all been brave," her voice, beautiful and lilting, corrected him. She looked right into his eyes; her gaze piercing his very soul. "It's not your fault. You can't prevent people from dying in war, but you can choose to keep fighting for their sake." Her eyes smiled at him; the way they sparkled seemed to be a silent language - one that said, "it will be alright," even when it wasn't. A language that spoke one word: kindness.

THE NURSE

She's so beautiful. So perfect. She doesn't belong in a place like here, he thought as she wrapped the last bandage around Ed's wound. He noticed how gently she touched him; the way she squeezed his hand so reassuringly, and the way she spoke words of encouragement to him.

"Can't you see he's dying?" Denni whispered hoarsely as she leaned over, gently tucking a blanket around his best friend. She looked at him and nodded slowly.

"We're doing all we can to save him," she replied, carefully wiping away the dried blood on his face with slow and soft movements. Then lowering her voice, she whispered, "but remember, even unconscious people can still hear what we're saying."

A deep groan caught the attention of the nurse. The soldier writhed around on his bed; his face twisted in pain. "Denni," his voice was barely a whisper, "thank you. I...I tried...be...brave." Beads of sweat laced his forehead.

Denni knelt beside him, tears running down his face. "I know you did, Ed. You were more brave than any of us." He tried to swallow the lump in his throat. "Just don't go, please." He grasped Ed's hand. You can't leave now. You're the only true friend I've got. Please, keep holding on."

Just talk to him. Keep him thinking.

"Ed, stay with me. Remember the day you gave Rilla the ring...she's still waiting for you. You can't die here...France isn't your home. You've always been a fighter, and that's not always bad. Please, you've got to keep fighting for her sake."

The young man squeezed his hand weakly. "I can't. I love her. I'm scared…help… m-m— " His eyes glazed over as his chest heaved and then fell, never to rise again.

Just wait, he'll breathe again. He has to.

Nothing.

He can't be gone.

Denni sat there in dazed shock.

He's gone? My best friend…gone?

Salty drops beaded his palms and his chest ached constantly. His throat felt tight as if he was trying to swallow a stone.

A hand touched his shoulder. He turned his head around, and locked eyes with the nurse. Her eyes were full of compassion, tinged with the ever-present gift of mercy.

"I'm sorry," she whispered. "I wish I could have saved him."

"But you never knew him. Why then?" He asked dumbly, trying to understand what she meant.

"Because every life is precious." She smiled faintly, a single tear rolling down her face.

"I know what it's like to lose someone dear to you - I lost my brother a few months ago."

So we've both lost someone through this war…we've both experienced pain. Denni stood to his feet as he looked at the young woman before him. "Thank you for trying… it means a lot," he paused. "And I'm sorry for your loss too."

She stared up at him. "I just wish I could have done more," she shook her head at the lifeless form lying in the bed. She looked up again, locking his gaze with such a gentle expression in those blue eyes. A slight smile wrinkled her lips; her face revealing the compassion she felt. "Over time, the hurt will heal," she promised as she walked away.

Denni watched the nurse as she left. He could still feel her soft touch on his shoulder. Her eyes so full of kindness.

And yet, his friend was gone.

CHAPTER TWO

The ground shuddered deeply; each movement as if the earth was trembling with fear. Chalky clouds hovered low across the gloomy land, waltzing slowly amongst the dusty-grey plumes of smoke. Ash-faced soldiers darted amongst the shadows. Two men crouched behind a mound, each bracing their grimy guns. Bullets whizzed overhead; too often a sickening thud or long, anguishing scream evidence of their mark. A grenade shot through the air, exploding as it hit the ground. Now only one man crouched behind the mound.

Sweat laced Denni's forehead.

Another dream.

He slowly pushed himself up, leaning against the dirt sides of the foxhole he was resting in. His gun lay ready beside him. His neck ached, and every muscle felt as if they had been entombed in a solid caste of iron.

Everything was deathly quiet; and yet he could still hear constant explosions and screams. Silence was something a soldier like him lost after hearing those sounds again and again.

"Lord, I don't understand. Why did he die, and not me?" he whispered, his voice barely audible. His stomach cramped; pain twisting it in tight knots. Parts of the dream drifted through his mind again...

Blood squirted from his side, spattering everywhere. The man's face was sickly white, each breath rasping against his lungs, and triggering another influx of life-giving liquid to pulse through the wound. Jagged pieces of shrapnel protruded from the skin.

Denni swallowed hard. His palms were wet against his face. He closed his eyes.

"Stay with me, Ed. We're gonna get you back safely. You'll be fine, I promise."

"I made a promise I couldn't keep, Lord. Ed's gone and so many others are dying too. How long until it's me lying cold under the ground?" The tears he wished he could feel weren't there. His throat felt dry.

"Lord, I know I broke my promise to Ed. I don't like going back on my word, but there are some things I just can't change. But I'm going to promise this to You - as soon as I get home, and as soon as this war is over, I'm never touching a weapon again in my life, to hurt someone else. I've done enough killing - and I hate it." His nails dug deep into his skin, breaking the surface.

"And that's a promise I'm going to keep."

§

The hospital was a dismal place. The only thing that cheered the atmosphere a little was the presence of the nurses; each in their own way, they tried to encourage the wounded soldiers as much as they were able. There was one nurse in particular who was known for her cheeriness and resolute spirit despite the circumstances.

She was slender in stature with auburn hair framing a delicate face, and her eyes, baby blue like the sky, seemed to always sparkle.

It had been a week since she had watched Ed die and tried somehow to comfort his grief-stricken friend. She'd noticed him a couple of times since then, quietly mourning his loss, but never trying to get attention.

She understood his pain; the memory of her brother still haunted her daily. It was for that reason that she had enlisted as a nurse in the first place - her brother's sacrifice was an inspiration that had heavily influenced her decision.

The cold wind enveloped her in an empty hug as she walked back to the hospital. Her eyes were fixed on a small grey book in her hands; the pages slightly blowing in the breeze. Red and black words marked each side. She closed her eyes, savouring the quiet moment.

Oh Lord, thank you for Your Word. It's the only thing giving me hope right now. She gently shut the book, returning it to a fold in her dress. *Every day seems the same; just more wounded people,* she thought as she entered the tent.

Rows of beds greeted her, each containing war-stricken patients. Several dreary faces brightened a little as she walked past, stopping now and then to encourage one of them.

A deep groan erupted from the farthest side of the room. She quickened her pace, and soon reached the soldier; his face was a blanket of white - a sharp contrast to his bloodshot eyes.

"It's alright," she murmured, carefully wiping a damp cloth across his sweaty brow.

"My arm, I can't feel it." His voice shook, trembling like his body. It didn't take long for her to notice - his left arm stopped at his elbow, wrapped heavily in bandages.

"I'm sorry," she faltered. "They had to remove it."

Disbelief clouded his face - "Gone?" He swallowed hard, trying to comprehend.

She nodded, trying somehow to comfort the poor soldier. "I know it might be hard now, but people will recognise your bravery in time to come - every scar is a reminder of the choice you made to fight for the freedom of others. You were very brave. I'll be back in a minute. Would you like a cup of tea?"

He nodded numbly; hardly taking notice of the question.

She smiled understandingly, and squeezed his right hand gently, trying to reassure the poor man. Then she left.

Another nurse met her as she stood near the tent

opening, slowly pouring the tea into the tin cup. Little spirals of steam twirled above the liquid.

"How is he doing?" The nurse's voice was distinctly French, each word softly accented. Concern filled her face.

"He's pretty shaken up since I told him. It must be so hard for him, Claire."

"Yes, it is. The other day he was telling me how he had proposed to a girl just before he left for war. I hope she'll still want him now, with one arm missing." Claire shook her head sadly.

"I feel so sorry for him." Her voice conveyed the pity she felt. "I better take this tea to him." She carried the steaming cup carefully back towards the cot, placing it gently into the soldier's hand.

"There you go. I'll be back to check on you soon," she said, offering the wounded man a warm smile before moving on to the next patient.

THE NURSE

CHAPTER THREE

"That should teach you not to mess with me." The tall bully landed a swinging blow, knocking Denni to the ground. He blinked hard, trying to ignore the salty taste in his mouth. Grimacing, he slowly pulled himself up again and faced the boy.

"Leave him alone." The stranger interjected; his voice was husky, with a powerful edge to it.

"Why?" The bully folded his arms defiantly, assuming a fighting stance.

"Because I said so."

"I don't care —" the boy started retorting, but something caught his attention and he quickly stopped. He shot a threatening glare at Denni, then ran off.

"Are you alright?" The stranger asked, his youthful eyes scanning Denni's bruised face.

"I'm fine...thank you for doing that."

The boy simply nodded, a wistful smile playing at his lips. "You're new here, aren't you?"

Denni shifted uneasily on his feet. "Yes, I am. My parents just *recently moved here, and I don't have any friends now."*

"I'll be your friend; I mean it. It's hard here at first, but you'll soon get used to it." He paused as if thinking for a moment. "What's your name?"

"I'm Denni. Thank you; I needed a friend. And your name is?" His eyes twinkled.

"I'm Ed."

Rain pelted down, saturating Denni as he trudged along the field. *"Are you alright?"* He could hear the voice so clearly. He'd heard that voice a thousand times. *I'm not alright now. If only I'd encouraged him not to enlist, he'd still be alive. But he would never have listened. "I'm your friend, Denni. True friends stick together. I want to serve my country too," he'd said as we enlisted together. It's all my fault.*

The bullets fell mercilessly upon the tired soldiers.

Oh Lord...why did he have to die? Why him?

Freezing drops of rain fell thick and fast, rapidly turning the ground into a trampled field of wet mud. Bolts of lightning flickered through the sombre sky. The once gentle slope up the hill was now a treacherous mudslide. Pools of blood mixed with the wet dirt, transforming the landscape into a reddy-brown bog. Bodies lay sinking into the miry terrain, some stretched across fallen trees, others entangled in barbed wire.

"Fall back, fall back," the officer shouted above the din as the Germans pressed hard against them. Slowly, step by step, driving them back across the lines.

Denni raced along the ground towards the enemy, ignoring the command of his officer. He had seen the young boy go down, after being shot by a German sniper. He couldn't leave him out there to die alone.

If Ed was here, he would be doing the same thing. But he's not; and I don't want him to die...not like Ed.

As he neared where the lad was lying, a small object flew through the air and landed by his leg. It was a metallic colour, dull like the grey clouds that hovered above.

He only noticed it when it was too late.

The explosion tore through his leg, mangling flesh and bone. He screamed in agony.

He could only just make out the form of the boy through the smoky haze but could hear nothing other than a deafening ringing between both ears.

If only...

Nausea overtook him, then all went black.

§

"Denni," the nurse gently shook him. Her Tennessean accent was a sad reminder of home; the only home he'd known since his English parents had decided to immigrate to America. He had enlisted to fight before America had publicly joined the war as a result of his British citizenship. It was a choice he felt he owed to his birth country. He opened his eyes slightly, trying to concentrate on the blurred figure before him. It was *her*.

Now everything would be fine.

But it wasn't.

Sunlight streamed in from the makeshift window, lighting up the long room. Rows of beds, occupied by men like him, filled the entirety of the area. Nurses worked tirelessly, caring for the wounded soldiers; their white uniforms brightening up the place a little.

He tried to sit up. Something felt different. Then he noticed it. The place where his right leg should have been was now just a stump, wrapped in a bandage the colour of cream.

"What happened? Where's my leg?" His eyes flitted around the room, full of fear.

A soft hand touched his shoulder. The nurse looked down at him, her face a mask of worry. "The explosion took your leg. They say you went to save that young boy."

She wiped the damp cloth tenderly across his forehead. Her very presence seemed to soothe his pain.

"Did...did he survive?" Denni looked at her face, trying to find some sort of answer.

She shook her head; her eyes mirroring the sorrow she felt. "No, he didn't. He lost too much blood. He was dead before we even reached him."

Denni clenched his hands together; ignoring the pain as

his nails dug into his dry skin. Grief clouded his face. "He's dead?" He stuttered. "All I wanted to do was save him; I just wanted another chance. Ed died because I couldn't save him in time. I wish he was still alive. And the boy; he was so young..." his thoughts trailed off.

"Please, Ed, don't go." His best friend's face was deathly pale - he'd seen something like that again recently. The boy. The dead boy.

Silence reigned for a moment; then the nurse nodded, her face grave and compassionate. "I'm so sorry." She paused, breathing in slowly. "I need to check on my other patients, but I'll come back later."

As she turned to leave, Denni called out to her, "I never actually found out your name?"

"Edith." She looked around and smiled sweetly.

THE NURSE

CHAPTER FOUR

Edith walked amongst the rows of simple beds, now and then offering a kindly word of encouragement or giving a much-needed dose of morphine.

As she neared the entrance to the tent, she noticed a young soldier leaning against the wall, watching her. She walked over and smiled at him. "Can I help you?"

"Oh, yes...please. Thank you. You *are* the nurse looking after Private Denni Alber, aren't you?" His eyes searched hers earnestly. His khaki uniform was damp and muddy, but his face still bore a courageous look that radiated throughout the rest of his demeanour.

"Yes, I am. And I understand you are a friend of his?" she replied, filling a cup of water.

The liquid was freezing cold.

So was the air around them.

Thunder rumbled in the distance, or maybe it was just the constant explosions that kept penetrating deep into the interior of the land.

"Yes, that's right. My name's Teddy. I helped carry his friend, Ed, here after he was wounded. I just wanted to check on him. The boys have been saying that he's lost his leg. Is that so?" The young man peered down the tent, trying to make out the figure of his friend.

Edith's smile faded. "Yes...we couldn't do anything. The explosion had done too much damage. He needs to rest now. Worrying is only going to make him worse."

A slither of sunlight broke through the stormy sky; a sign that there was still hope even in this blood-stained world. Edith looked back towards where Denni lay. She shook her head sadly. "It's just terrible how people are losing so much because of another's greed."

Teddy nodded slowly. "Yes...thank you for your help. Please give him my regards when he wakes."

"I'll make sure I pass that message on. There's nothing worse for a soldier than having to sit and rest while his comrades keep on fighting." She watched as the young man left the tent, making his way through the soldiers that stood gathered around.

The ground shook as another explosion went off nearby.

Screams flooded the air. *More wounded soldiers*, she thought, returning to her duties inside the tent.

When she checked on Private Denni that evening, she found him sleeping deeply. It wasn't often that front-line soldiers were able to sleep, so she left him in his present relief. The sky above her was a blur of smoke and stars as she walked back towards the nurses' quarters. In the distance, enemy fire ruptured the night air.

The Lord is my Shepherd, I shall not want. The familiar verse echoed through her mind, giving her comfort.

THE NURSE

CHAPTER FIVE

She closed the grey book, her eyes resting for a moment on the cross stitched carefully into the cover. *Lord, help me to be a blessing to someone today. Use me for your glory.* Slowly rising, she nestled the book under her pillow and headed outside towards the hospital tent.

The doctor glanced at her as she walked in, his face marked with weariness. A slight smile creased his lips as she walked up. "You're always ready to help, Edith. I appreciate knowing I can rely on you."

"Just doing my job, sir." She scanned the room, her eyes resting upon a soldier who was quietly watching her from where he lay in his cot. A shadow of a smile crept across her face as she walked toward him.

"How are you feeling today, Denni?" She carefully unwrapped the bandages around the stump that used to be his leg. The sigh of relief that escaped her lips was hardly audible, but the way his eyes lit up was clear it hadn't gone unnoticed.

"How is my leg?" His voice was earnest, almost wistful.

"It's doing fine. There's no infection at the moment." She gently wound a fresh bandage around his leg, pausing for a moment as her eyes caught sight of a small black book tucked partially under the pillow.

"Is that a Bible?"

A smile curled his lips as he pulled the book out. "Yes, it is. And I'm so glad I have it out here."

Edith nodded; her eyes sparkling. "Same - I don't know how people go through this war without trusting in God."

"We have something they don't - hope." He spoke quietly, but the joy in his voice was unmistakable.

"Yes, we do," she murmured.

And I've found someone who shares this hope, he thought, watching as she walked to the next cot.

§

Bullets cascaded through the air finding their mark on random victims. Death was ever-present on this blood-bathed grave of fallen heroes.

"*Medic...we need a medic!*" Screams pierced the air. Shadows darted in and out of the hazy field. Two soldiers dashed through the groups of men bravely fighting against the odds. They carried a man between them. His restless form lay on the stretcher, his legs a mangled mess. Heaving with exhaustion, they pushed up the hillside.

§

Back inside the hospital, Edith knelt on the ground, carefully wrapping a bandage around a soldier's arm. "There you go." Her tone was soothing, but it couldn't take away the fear behind his eyes.

Several voices clashed together outside, dragging her attention toward the entrance. She quickly rose and headed towards the disturbance. A couple of soldiers stumbled along the ground, trying their best to keep the stretcher steady.

She was ready as she met them, quickly slipping a pill into the wounded soldier's mouth. "Let's get him into the tent. If we are going to save him, we must work fast."

"Doctor! This man needs immediate attention!" Edith gestured towards the stretcher, whose occupant was writhing in pain.

"Here boys, bring him this way." The doctor grabbed his surgeon's kit; the soldiers followed quickly behind.

The nurses hastened after them, ready to assist.

One of the younger ones shook her head sadly, a confused look painting her face. "There's so much pain and hurt out here. I just don't understand why God lets this happen." Her tone was refined, each word perfectly pronounced; her English heritage was no secret. Though tall with an air of maturity which must have helped convince the enlisting officers, she must have only been around sixteen.

"I often ask myself the same question. But then, I remember that God is loving, He is merciful, but He also allows these things to happen to test us. It's not that He takes pleasure in letting hundreds of people die." Edith looked straight into the young woman's eyes. She could see the fear. A single drop of sorrow descended down her cheek. "The *only* thing we can do and the *best* thing we can do is *trust* God."

The nurse nodded slowly. Even among such horror and carnage, they were *not* alone.

§

17 December 1940.

It's 10pm, Tuesday; seven days before Christmas. I find it ironic that at a time when we would normally be celebrating joy and good tidings, the world is torn in two by war and the greed of one man. I've been struggling lately with my feelings. There is a nurse stationed here, and I've found myself growing rather fond of her. Since I lost my leg, she's been the one to take care of me. I'm sure she feels the same way about me, but I want to be careful. I've seen so many of the other boys fall helplessly in love with nurses here, but the reality is that many of us won't survive this war. I don't want to commit myself to another person, without knowing it's meant to be. It's hard though.

I want a companion beside me; someone I can share my fears and worries with. Lord, help me to know if she is the right one. Help me to be disciplined with my feelings. I've always loved You Lord, but now I realize more than ever how much I need to rely on you for everything. It's so hard to stay true to my convictions when I'm surrounded by friends who are forsaking You. There's so much sin going on around me. I want to stay true to You. Help me, Lord, to trust You, and please, give me peace in my heart concerning Edith.

Denni closed the small leather journal; its edges scarred by years of use. A slight sigh escaped his lips.

THE NURSE

CHAPTER SIX

Wind danced along the ground, gathering leaves the colour of fire on its way. Ominous clouds breathed icy drops of rain, spattering them down on the land. Thunder rolled in the distance, flickering bursts of light forewarning of the coming storm.

A curtain of smoke hung low over the dreary barracks. The sky was as bleak as the faces of the men crouching around the fires. Joy was a lost emotion out here. It had been long buried with the first few victims of the War.

A crow perched on the rooftop of one of the buildings; its beady eyes scanning the landscape before it. Black feathers ruffled in the wind; a haunting yet true reminder of the dead.

Edith sat leaning against a brick wall that had partly crumbled into the ground beneath. The once cheerful white of her dress was now buried beneath a covering of mud, dust, and blood. She sat silently; eyes closed, and hands folded in her lap. Solitude wasn't easy to find.

Lord, You know how I've always been dedicated to waiting until You show me the right man. I feel like he's here. I'm struggling with my feelings towards him; yes, he's handsome and all that, but more so, I find his faith and trust in You so attractive. Lord, help me not to fall in love with him until I know he's the one. Help me guard my feelings, and let me not reveal any interest in him until he's shown that towards me. I want to wait for him. It's so easy to want to be loved, and want companionship out here, because the truth is, I'm lonely. So many of the girls here are forsaking You and letting their feelings control their actions. I don't want to be like that, Lord. Help me!

The thud of footsteps close by broke the silence.

"We need a nurse, please." Voices rang through the air, tugging Edith back to reality. She jumped up and headed towards the disruption.

Two soldiers were stumbling towards the hospital carrying their wounded companion.

"Here, let me help him," she told them as she slipped the drug into the poor boy's mouth. His blue eyes shook with fear; drops of perspiration mixed with blood trickling down the side of his face.

He looked familiar, or maybe it was simply that he reminded her of her own brother. Memories flickered through her mind, a haunting replay of the past.

"Edith, I've decided to study in England," he had told her one day, as they walked home together from church. "Of course, I'll miss you all terribly, but I do think it's a splendid opportunity."

The memory faded and was quickly replaced by another dismal one. *She clasped the letter tightly, the words ringing in her ears. "I enlisted today - I know I'm not British, but I don't feel right seeing all of my English friends go off to war, and I stay back. I hope you don't hate me for it. I spent the most part of last night praying about it, and I feel it's the right thing to do."*

"Nurse, are you alright?" One of the soldiers was staring at her with a concerned expression. He pointed to the wounded boy. "What about him?"

"Let's get him into the hospital." she urged, as the young soldier slipped into a state of unconsciousness. Instinctively, she checked his pulse and paused. A look of grief painted her face as she looked at the other men. "I'm sorry..."

"There's a letter from the army." The young post boy handed the envelope over, a friendly smile cast upon his face. She glanced at the official-looking seal stamped upon it; her heart faltering, knowing all too well what it meant. Ripping it open quickly, her eyes barely read the first few lines. "We regret to inform you that Private Jamie Blately was killed in action on 13 October 1939. We are very sorry for your loss."

She opened her eyes, her gaze resting softly upon the dead boy.

The soldiers glanced around in numb shock, gently lowering the stretcher. "He shouldn't even have been here. He was only a boy."

"I know...this war is destroying so many young people. I hate seeing so much death everywhere." She stood up slowly, wiping her bloodied hands on her apron.

War revealed the best and the worst of mankind; and it was something she saw every day.

The grey sky was like the tears that fell so freely on that battlefield. Bleak and cold; just like the piles of unnamed heroes who lay entombed in the miry terrain.

She headed towards the hospital and resumed her duties.

CHAPTER SEVEN

Over the next few weeks, Edith visited Denni every day. As the days went by, their love for deep conversations fuelled their growing interest in one another. As their relationship grew so did the painful realization that Denni was no longer able to serve his country. Their afternoon talks swiftly changed to pondering the future before them. Drawn together by their faith, and similarities, Denni and Edith knew the sobering reality that lay ahead, and the thought of separation weighed heavily upon them.

§

The moonlight cast a gentle glow over the weather-beaten barracks. Stars twinkled overhead, now and then hiding behind the wisps of smoke that hung low over the terrain. In some of the buildings, windows were entirely blown out, the effect caused by routine explosions. Sharp shards of glass were buried amongst the loose soil.

Edith sat in the doorway of one of these buildings, her

hair waving gently in the breeze. A small brown book nestled in her lap.

A dark shadow hobbled towards her.

She smiled to herself.

Denni limped into the entranceway, attempting to sit down. A pair of crutches accompanied him; paint peeling from the constant use. His blonde hair stood out in the darkness around them.

"Teddy said you were here," he cleared his throat. His hands were shaking. "Edith," he suddenly grabbed her hand, looking straight into her eyes. His mind was like a whirlpool; and it wasn't easy to steady his fears.

Just calm down.

"I want to ask you something that is probably going to be hard to hear."

Just get on with it.

"I'm sure you've already figured out that I won't be staying here for too much longer," he paused.

Blast it! Why can't I just say what I mean?

Edith looked at him inquisitively.

"Over the last two months, I've been spending a lot of time praying about the future. You see, when I think about life after the war, I see two paths, joined together. Ever since I first met you, I haven't been able to get you off my mind. I've tried forgetting you, because I don't want to give my heart to you knowing that we may never be able to spend the rest of our lives together; but I *can't* forget you." He inhaled deeply.

"Yes?" She blushed slightly, her cheeks a soft crimson.

"When I am discharged, would you consider...no, not consider...*please* ask to leave too?"

Her eyes widened. "Me? Leave *here*? Oh, Denni, I'm not sure if that's possible. I mean, I don't want to leave here, knowing other people are fighting and nursing and that I'm just sitting back at home doing nothing." Concern was written all across her face. She twisted her fingers, entwining them in the folds of her skirt. "It's not that I don't like you; I do...I like you a lot. But we haven't committed to anything yet, and I can't just go asking to be discharged without a valid reason. They *need* us nurses here...I think our presence calms the men down a bit," She paused, looking ever so softly into his eyes. "I don't want you to feel like I'm saying no to you."

"Edith, please, I love you. I *do*."

"But I'm needed out here!"

"But there's other nurses. Surely, you can leave?"

"I can't. I'm not going too."

She could see the disappointment growing on his face.

"Denni, I want you to know something. I don't want you to think that I'm staying out here because I'm trying to prove myself. Or like I'm trying to be some strong woman. I hate it out here. I feel like I've seen so much death that

I've almost lost any emotion towards those who've died. It's tested my faith more than ever before. I just don't feel right about leaving them out here and going back to safety." Tears begged to come, and she let them.

He sighed. "I know. Please, promise me *one* thing. Will you pray about it? Ask God for His guidance during this time. And I'll do the same. Not just about this, but about us. I want to do this right. "

"So do I. I will pray."

He rose, leaning on his crutches. As he hobbled back towards the barracks, he turned around. "Thank you."

CHAPTER EIGHT

One afternoon the commanding officer came to visit Denni. He was a tall man, with a friendly, easy-going manner. "Hello, it's Private Denni, right?" He smiled kindly, yet something in his face betrayed that he was the bearer of bad news.

"Yes sir, that's me." Denni nodded slightly.

The officer twisted his hands and muttered something under his breath. "I guess you've probably figured it out already, but you've been discharged due to the loss of your leg. I came not only to tell you but also to thank you for your heroic actions and immense bravery out there on the lines. I'm sorry to let you go - you're one of the best we have." He paused, a faraway look in his eyes. "You'll be sent home on the next ship. It's due to leave in about two days. Godspeed, Private Denni Alber." He saluted and walked away.

Denni leaned back with an audible groan. *Oh God, please let Edith come back with me. Please! God help me!* The poor soldier poured out his heart in a silent prayer. Tears that had previously refused to come now flowed freely down his face.

A gentle tap on his shoulder sent a little thrill through his bones but was almost instantly replaced by a pang of sorrow that swept across him like a wave in the sea.

Edith looked into his eyes, her face revealing that she knew what he had been told. "How long until you leave?" she asked, slightly choking on her words.

"In about two days." His face was a mask of worry.

"Oh Denni, I don't know what to say. You know how much I feel for you. I've prayed and begged so hard for God to show me what to do. I just don't know!" Tears raced down her cheek, each one competing against the other.

"I've been praying too! Please remember this though - just because you don't feel like God has answered your prayers doesn't mean He's ignoring you. Maybe you haven't heard His answer because it's not the one you *want* to hear."

"But what do I do?"

"Ask if you can! Ask to be discharged! I'll be worried sick about you. I can't just leave here, knowing that the one I love is in danger! *Please*, Edith?" The soldier grasped her hand, looking into her eyes tenderly. She could see the anguish in his face.

"For *your* sake, I will ask. You know I love you too!" She

whispered, her voice like a sorrowful song. Her cheeks were wet, and her hair ruffled, but to him, she looked as beautiful as ever.

"But what if the doctor says no?" She added.

Denni looked into her eyes and swallowed hard. "Then if that happens, we will know that it's not God's will."

He squeezed her hand reassuringly.

She nodded slowly, then left.

THE NURSE

CHAPTER NINE

"I'm sorry, but I cannot fulfil your request. We need all the help we can get out here on the front lines. You are one of the best nurses we have." The tall man shook his head dolefully. Red stains decorated his uniform. "I can't afford to lose you now."

"But doctor, there's a soldier who's being dispatched because he can't fight anymore. We've become rather fond of each other. It's breaking his heart to know that I'll still be here!"

"I understand that...but my decision remains the same. In a world where all hope is dying, we need all the help we can get. I'm sorry." He smiled kindly, trying somehow to comfort the poor woman before him.

"Yes, sir. I understand. Thank you for taking the time to listen to me." She tried to sound grateful, but her words were thick with pain.

So this is it? O God, you know this is not what I want. Give me the strength to endure, and please Lord, help Denni. He's struggling so hard, trying to trust You. The reality that she would be here without him was not a pleasant thought. Neither was the reality of war.

§

Late that night, Edith pulled the small grey book out from underneath her coat. Its cover was faded and slightly torn, but the stitched cross was still visible. She turned the first page, slowly flicking through each until she reached Isaiah. Her eyes hovered over the words, searching for comfort.

"Fear not, for I am with you; be not dismayed, for I am your God; I will strengthen you, I will help you, I will uphold you with my righteous right hand."

Tears fell gently down her cheeks. *But how, God? How can I not fear, when everything I love is being pulled away from me? I don't know how to tell Denni.* Her lips quivered. Sorrow shook her body. *Be not dismayed...I will strengthen you.* The words echoed around her mind.

God, help me to not be dismayed. Help me to trust in You. I need You, tonight, more than ever before. Her eyelids felt heavy, and she let them take over. Sleep tenderly gathered her in its arms, gently rocking her in time to the lullaby of gunshots and explosions that haunted the air outside.

Over in the soldiers' sleeping quarters, the moon shone brightly, casting a warm glow across the dreary buildings. A soldier awkwardly knelt on the ground. A pair of crutches lay in the soil beside him. His hands were clasped together, and his face stared upwards. The sky above him was a glittering array of stars playing hide and seek behind the thin clouds of smoke passing by.

"Father, I need Your help. You already know what Edith's been told, but I don't. I don't know if she's going or staying; and Lord, that's testing my faith. You know how much I care for her, and my desire to protect her, but I can't do that back at home. Please, Lord, if the answer is no, please protect her out here. Give her strength to endure this war, and most of all, Lord, keep her close to You. The only way she'll get through this is by holding on to You." As he looked into the night sky, his face was edged by the eerie light that haunted the dark and deathly field. He picked up his crutches and slowly stood up. Pain encumbered each step of his way as he hobbled inside.

THE NURSE

CHAPTER TEN

Edith's last visit with Denni was agonising. Even though he still had a day until the ship departed, the dock was a good day's journey away, forcing him to leave sooner than expected.

"Edith, before you tell me what the doctor said, I want to tell you something. *I love you*, no matter what happens. Even if we are separated for the time being, or even…" he paused, and held her hand, "even if one of us should die, God has brought us together, and that is something that distance cannot break. I'm trusting God in this, Edith, and I pray that He gives you the same peace."

"I've been praying about this ever since that evening, Denni. I still didn't have peace about asking, but I did it because I know it's my responsibility to be willing to do whatever the Lord wants me to do." She faltered, not wanting to carry on. Her hands trembled in his.

Denni nodded, waiting patiently to hear what he already had figured out. He smiled gently at her, whispering,

"It's ok...I understand."

She swallowed hard, breathing in deeply. "I would have come with you, but the doctor said no. I *tried*! I have peace that it's not God's will for me to leave. My heart's breaking knowing that I'm staying though! I love you, too!" She held onto his hand, not wanting to let go.

He looked straight at her, a single tear rolling down his cheek. "I know you tried, and I have peace too. *Someone* once wisely told me that we can't prevent things like this from happening, but we can *choose* to keep fighting for their sake," he winked at her.

A shadow of a smile flickered across her face. "I wish we could go through this together though."

"I know. I wish it too...with *all* my heart." His big brown eyes glistened in the early morning sun.

"Excuse me, Private, the truck's ready to take you. The sergeant said to tell you." The soldier's words interrupted their goodbyes as he waited patiently for Denni's reply.

"Thank you...please tell him that I'll be there in a minute." He smiled cheerfully at the young man, a stark contrast to what he truly felt.

As the soldier walked away, Edith placed her hand tenderly on his arm. Looking straight into his eyes, she whispered, "I love you."

Denni could almost feel his heart tearing in two.

This might be the last time.

"Edith, I have one last thing to give you." He leaned down on his crutches, in an attempt to kneel. The sunrise behind them created a beautiful silhouette. "It's not fancy, or pretty...but it's all I have," he paused, and looked up at her, staring into those gorgeous eyes.

She gasped as he revealed a ring formed from the metal shell casing of a bullet. The two lines of the ring entwined at one end.

"Will you be my wife?"

Her smile almost answered the question before she uttered a word. "Oh, Denni! Yes, oh yes!"

"I guess it symbolises how our paths met. And how God brought us together," he added, overjoyed with her answer. "Promise me you'll come home to me?" he asked ever so earnestly.

"I *do* promise...with all my heart."

"I have to go," he whispered, pulling her close to him. "I love you, Edith." He gently placed a kiss on her cheek.

"I love you too. Goodbye, *my* love."

THE NURSE

CHAPTER ELEVEN

The next weeks were like a whirlwind, leaving no time for sorrow or reliving memories. Grief was like a shadow, following Edith wherever she went. War was Grief's slave, continually providing a new victim. The only true friend War had was Death, who was never satisfied, even with the hundreds of souls that War presented.

For Edith, the battlefield was a constant reminder of Denni. *There he was, standing there, giving her the only flower left on this broken land. His smiling face looking into her eyes. The gentle arm around her shoulder.*

Then he was gone; a fleeting memory swept away by the reality around her.

Oh God, I can't keep going on like this. This war is killing me! And hundreds others. I'm trying to trust You, but it's so hard not having Denni here to keep reminding me of Your goodness. Lord, help me!

§

The wisp of a moon peeked through the smoky clouds as if it was too frightened to cast its eerie light across the death-strewn field. Small shadows scurried over the broken ground, now and then stopping beside the body of a fallen soldier and nibbling at the dirty flesh. Unnamed heroes lay almost unrecognisable, forever marred by the work of nature and mankind alike.

A crow perched upon a small form, pecking at the charred soldier. In the trenches lights gently flickered. Voices murmured. Men sat in groups, huddled around small fires, shivering in their bloodied uniforms. A sergeant lifted a cigarette to his lips, slowly lighting it.

Inside the nurses' quarters, Edith sat at a makeshift desk, squinting in the dim light. A single piece of paper lay before her, and besides that, a small pen. A row of cots stood in the room; threadbare blankets neatly folded over them. A few personal possessions rested on the beds reminding their owners of home.

She picked up the pen. Her fingers shook slightly with the cold wind that was creeping through the slits in the barracks. A drop of black ink scarred the paper.

Dear Denni,

Oh, how I miss you. I long to see your face again. I'm sorry I didn't write back to you sooner. The past few weeks have been the worst days of my life. The Germans have been trying harder than ever to push us back. So many soldiers coming in with wounds so awful that I don't think half of them will even make it. Most of them are suffering from shock. I've never had to stitch someone up as fast as I'm doing nowadays. One boy was brought in yesterday; the whole left side of his face was torn almost off. They said he had tried to cover a grenade to protect the others. We tried as hard as we could to save him but despite our efforts, he didn't make it. Oh Denni, I cried so hard last night. He was only about fourteen. I'm struggling out here without you. I know God is keeping me safe, but I can't keep doing this. I'm losing my mind. This war...it's taking so many people. I feel like I'm constantly living in a nightmare. There are bodies everywhere, so mutilated and mangled, and I'm seeing them every day. Denni, how I wish I could come home to you! I'm trying to remember that the Lord is my Shepherd, but honestly, I'm struggling to see God's hand in all this. I need your prayers, dearest. Every night, before I try to sleep, I look at my ring, and I can see you in my mind. I love you, Denni.

I hope you're well.

With all the love my heart can send,

Your Edith.

She gently folded the paper. A small drop fell onto the envelope. "O God, help me," she whispered, walking back out into the dark night air and heading downhill towards the medical station they had set up behind the trenches.

An explosion lit the sky, outlining the silent forms stretched across the ground. Another closely followed. Machine guns tore through the smoky haze. Screams pierced the air that had been so quiet just a minute ago.

"Get down! Get down!" The sergeant roared through the cigarette still in his mouth. Blood spattered down his uniform, and he fell into the oozing mud.

"Grenade!" A dull grey object spun through the sooty-black air, landing beside a soldier busily attempting to lift his wounded companion. Terror flickered through his eyes as he realized his fate.

An ear-piercing sound temporarily deafened those nearby as the shockwave knocked Edith to the ground. Her ears were ringing; constantly repeating the sound.

Over and over again.

The soldier now lay writhing on the torn-up ground, trying somehow to escape the excruciating pain that was wracking every inch of what was left of his body. His legs were a bloodied pulp, victims of a weapon so small and yet so vicious. Unable to move, he could only try to drag himself towards safety. His friend was no more.

Smoke wrapped around the trenches as soldiers cautiously ran through the haze. Shrapnel hurtled through the air. Explosions cast an eerie glow across the field of death.

"Help me! Please!" The soldier was close. She could hear

him. The path was dangerous, but she knew her duty.

It might not be protocol for me to go, but he needs help.

"Hold on, I'm coming." Her reassuring reply gave the poor soldier small relief.

Foul mud oozed through her boots as she stumbled along the trench, awkwardly trying to pull a painkiller from the satchel swinging wildly around her waist.

Bodies, marred by the tools of War, were strewn everywhere, blood still dripping from their recent victims. Rats scurried out of her way.

A body lay in her path, fresh blood staining the mud. Smoke curled up in gentle spirals from a cigarette lying on the ground beside him.

The soldier saw her coming. And so did a sniper, hidden by the smoky haze that shrouded the field. He adjusted his sights, levelling his gun as the nurse stooped down beside the bloodied half-form of a man.

She grabbed the drug, and shoved it under his tongue; his eyes shaking with fear.

The sniper pulled his trigger.

THE NURSE

CHAPTER TWELVE

"Come," the short soldier signalled to the others. "Over here." He stood over two motionless bodies, drenched by the heavy rain. A couple soldiers walked over.

"Alfie, that's a nurse!" One of the two remarked somewhat gravely.

Alfie gently placed two fingers on her neck. "Roger, I can feel a pulse. It's faint, but it's there alright. Help me lift her up," he paused, then added, "be careful, though. We don't know how badly she's wounded."

Roger nodded slowly. "This war…" he sighed.

As they gently picked her up, a slight moan drew their attention to the man beside her. The other soldier, who appeared to be their sergeant, knelt down by him.

"He's not going to make it; we have to leave him because we can't take both of them." His tone sounded compassionate, with a slight release of emotion in those words.

"Let's get this girl back quickly, before the Germans start again," urged the Sergeant.

THE NURSE

They picked their way quickly across the torn land, carrying the nurse as carefully as they could. Blood lay in pools everywhere. The stench of dead bodies was almost unbearable. Twisted barbed wire entangled the remains of the unfortunate.

A crow sat upon the stump of a burnt tree; an ironic reminder of beauty and carnage. Its wail was a haunting tribute to the fallen yet its desire for flesh so detestable.

§

Ribbons of fiery red laced the evening sky, entwining with golden clouds. For any passer-by who hadn't been around the last two years, it would be almost impossible to comprehend the events that had occurred. The sky was a stark contrast to reality, however.

War was here, stealing the lives of so many men and women. For some, the end came quickly, almost instantly. For others, they lay alone on the cold field, as they waited until death came and took them.

Shrouds of mist crept across the ground. Shadows twirled along the hill. Voices murmured through the air.

Back in the barracks, a few lights cast a warm glow across the rows of small buildings. Piles of bricks lay crumbled upon the earth. Several nurses hurried over towards the hospital area; worried looks painted across their faces. Their uniforms resembled the work they had to do.

"Is it true?"

"Is she badly hurt?"

"Will she be okay?"

Their voices mixed together in a rush of questions as the doctor appeared. His brow was furrowed and the look in his eyes was distant.

"I've removed the bullet, but she's lost a fair bit of blood. I think we're going to need a transfusion. I'm just trying to find someone who would be a suitable donor."

The women shook their heads sadly.

"Excuse me, doctor, but what is Edith's blood type?" One of the younger nurses stepped forward, her eyebrows raised inquisitively.

The doctor stared at the girl before him and sighed, "O negative, unfortunately."

A gleam of hope appeared in the girl's eyes. "But sir, my blood type is O. Can she have mine?"

He stared at her for a second; "We'll do our best."

"Oh, thank you, doctor. She's helped me a lot during this war." Her lips quivered slightly as tears formed in her eyes. "I hope it will work."

"Follow me, and we'll see what we can do."

THE NURSE

CHAPTER THIRTEEN

A couple of nurses met them at the door.

White caps covered their hair. Blood stained their uniforms.

"Doctor, have you found anyone yet?" one of them asked, searching his eyes for an answer.

He nodded in the direction of the young nurse. "Yes, I have."

"Oh! So young!" she gasped. "But surely—"

"I know, but she's the only one who offered. We've got to try."

The woman sighed softly. "Alright, I'll get the table ready." She motioned to the girl. "This way, please."

They entered another room, the walls a dull grey colour. If you could associate colours with feelings, it looked as if they had been painted in Grief. A small bed lay in one corner. On the other side, a table rested; several medical instruments were spread across the rough wood, and a roll of bandages had been placed inside a square tray.

"So, what's your name?" The woman asked kindly, after sitting the girl down on the edge of the bed.

"Lily Porter." She smiled. Her soft brown eyes twinkled in the evening light that was seeping through the window.

"Well, Lily, you seem like a very brave young woman," the old nurse remarked as she set everything up. She slipped a needle into the girl's arm and her blood began to flow. Lily looked away with a shiver.

"What's the matter, dearie? You see blood every day. Why turn away now?" The nurse's smile was soothing.

"I know I do; it's just, I'm not used to seeing that much of my own," she answered nervously. "You see, the truth is, I don't like blood. I struggle seeing it every day."

"I understand. It's not right that you should be seeing the things you do, especially at your age." She gently pulled the needle out, instantly replacing it with a small cotton ball.

"Now, you shouldn't walk or do anything that requires physical movement for the next few hours. Your body needs to have time to replace the blood you've just given. I'm sure this will do Edith a lot of good. Just rest quietly on this bed; someone will come for you later."

The young nurse lay back; her face was pale, but her eyes still sparkled. Her eyelids hung heavy, and sleep was a precious gift out here. Soon, the only thing audible in that room was her delicate breathing.

Edith lay on the hard cot, as the last few drops of blood travelled through the tube into her arm. The nurse smiled kindly at her as she gradually regained consciousness.

"Why am I here? What happened?" Pain gnawed at her side.

"You were shot; you lost a lot of blood."

Memories flashed through her mind; the last couple of days piecing together slowly. *She grabbed the drug, and shoved it under his tongue, his eyes were filled with fear.* "The soldier...the one I tried to help. Is...is he...fine?"

The nurse shook her head. "I'm sorry, they had to leave him. He wasn't going to make it."

Edith groaned slightly. "He was in so much pain," she whispered. "Who donated their blood to me?" Her voice was weak. A dull ache throbbed at the back of her head.

"The youngest nurse here, Lily Porter. She was very keen to help. If it weren't for her, you might be in a lot more trouble."

Recognition flashed across Edith's face. "Oh, please thank her for me," she whispered, trying not to let the lump in her throat take over.

"I will, and you better take it easy," said the nurse, squeezing her hand gently.

Weak as she was, Edith smiled back at the nurse.

THE NURSE

CHAPTER FOURTEEN

Soldiers moved quickly among the barracks, stumbling and splashing through the muddy puddles. The moonlight sent shimmering shadows dancing across the pools of water collecting on the dark ground. Hushed whispers sang a harmony with the distant thud of explosions.

Inside the headquarters, several men stood around a long, weathered table. The edges were chipped, and several scratches drew lines along the surface. A map stretched across it; little red pins penetrating specific points on the chart.

One of the soldiers, the general judging by his uniform, pointed at the map in earnest haste. His eyes scanned the presentation before him.

"Gentlemen, I have received word that we are to retreat. The Germans are proving too strong an adversary for us at this stage, and we cannot afford to lose more men by a lapse of judgement. We must leave tonight."

A murmur of mixed feelings interrupted him. The men glanced at each other with startled expressions.

"Arrangements have already been made for half our company to leave in the next hour. It will primarily include the wounded. We will need to work speedily and efficiently in order to leave before we are noticed."

"Yes, sir!" The unanimous answer brought relief to the General. The expressions of his men had not gone unnoticed.

"Lieutenant Randon, please send the doctor to me."

"Yes, sir. Right away, sir," the lieutenant replied as he speedily left the room and hastened towards the hospital.

CHAPTER FIFTEEN

Dark figures ducked in and out of the buildings. Several carried stretchers between them; on some, the occupants writhed and groaned in pain, but on others, there was no motion.

Nurses rushed back and forth, aiding in helping the wounded soldiers reach the trucks.

Edith was one of the first to be carried to the vehicles waiting to leave. Two young soldiers had assisted her, both of whom she recognised as previous patients. They reminded her of her own dead brother. The brother she'd never been able to say goodbye to. Tears formed in her eyes as memories filled her mind.

Hushed voices urged the soldiers on. Soon, the trucks were loaded, and their engines began to rumble. The wheels spun in the thick mud, spattering it everywhere. The men dug their feet into the ground, pushing against the vehicles with all their strength. Wet dirt oozed through their weathered boots.

Slowly, the trucks gave way, and step by step, the soldiers moved them towards firmer land. Spirals of smoke from the exhaust pipes twirled in the light breeze as the vehicles roared to life.

Scurrying shadows feasted out on the battlefield. Sober faces watched the darkness outside, waiting for their time to leave.

And so, an hour passed.

§

A steady rumble pierced the distance. As it grew closer, forms appeared in the sky, outlined by a vivid moon splash. Several engines groaned in the sky as a group of fighter planes dived through the night air. Flinging dark shadows across the ground, they headed towards the barracks.

Nurses and soldiers alike raced outside to their doom. Flashes of light lit up the sky as the planes released an overload of bombs upon the quiet buildings. The explosions tore through the walls and bricks, crumbling everything in their paths.

Over near the hospital, Lily woke to the chaos around her. Her body felt weak. She stumbled out of her bed. Blood rushed to her head, and she fell on the hard floor. Fear gripped her.

'Help me, please! Somebody, help me! I can't escape,

please!" She screamed and cried as she tried in vain to get up again.

An ear-piercing noise screeched through the air and slammed into the building opposite her. Glass shattered across the floor, breaking in a thousand pieces. Dust and smoke twirled above flames as they licked at the walls.

"Lord, help me! Please!" she begged as she dragged herself over to the far end of the room, trying to escape the danger.

She could hear the screams…

A heavy thud, followed instantly by an explosion, hit the room, and everything went black.

THE NURSE

CHAPTER SIXTEEN

The morning light peeped through the curtain of smoke that hung heavy in the air. Survivors stumbled over piles of crumbling bricks and charred wood. Shards of glass were buried amongst the ruins.

A few nurses and several soldiers were the only ones left here; their fate unknown. Dust covered their faces and fear lurked in their eyes.

Glowing embers huddled in smoking piles between the blackened remains. The odd flame fed hungrily on what was left of the barracks.

Death was an ever-present shadow that lurked around here, just like the crow from the battlefield perched on the half-crushed form of a table. Beady eyes scanned the wreckage. Its song was a dull melody accompanied by the quiet sobs that throbbed in every heart present.

Soldiers once audacious now stood depleted of all energy. Life had been sucked from them and replaced with fear.

All had suffered one way or another in the slaughter of the previous night. For some, dark bruises and minor scratches were their lot, but for those who had tried to save their fellow companions, their wounds were far greater. Deep gashes, tarnished by dust and mud, clad one courageous man. His face was singed and marred by a painful burn he had received whilst attempting to rescue his wounded friend.

"Over here, quick!" The voice urged, causing the strongest of the party to obey. One of the men bent down near the area they had once called a hospital. His hands feebly clutched the wood and bricks, trying to pull them away.

"There's a nurse here...come on, help." They scrambled over the piles of rubble and lifted the beams. The still form of the old nurse lay buried amongst the ruins; dust covered her uniform.

They gently lifted her out from the carnage and laid her down on the ground.

"She's still breathing," the man replied, feeling her pulse.

Her eyelids fluttered open. "Lily," she whispered weakly. "Is she alright?" Her side heaved with slow painful breaths.

The group looked at each other with haunted expressions. Their eyes said everything.

"She didn't make it," one of the other nurses faltered. Tears drew faulty lines through the dust on her cheeks.

The older lady's face was pinched with agony and sorrow.

"I tried...rescue her..." her voice trembled. Then her eyes closed. She took one final breath, savouring the last moment of her life.

Then everything stopped.

Grief came swiftly to the victims in that deserted town.

THE NURSE

CHAPTER SEVENTEEN

"Sir, may I come in?" The young officer knocked at the door, worry lines creasing his face. The corridor in which he stood was long and painted white. Doors to several other rooms lined the hallway. A few nurses stood in the doorway of one of these, talking in hushed whispers.

"Come in," the voice inside replied. The officer walked in and stood to attention. The room was small with just a few pieces of simple furniture. A desk rested in one corner and behind that, sitting in a hard, straight-backed chair, was the General.

"What's the matter, Lieutenant Randon?" He folded his hands and looked inquiringly at the young man.

"The Germans launched a surprise air-attack two nights ago at our previous base. Several survivors have managed to reach the nearest town safely but most of the remaining soldiers and nurses were killed," his voice quivered. "Sir, one of them was my fiancée."

The General's countenance was masked with emotion,

despite his attempts to keep his face rigid. "Thank you, Lieutenant Randon, for informing me. I'm sorry for your loss." He sighed deeply after clearing his throat.

"It's alright, Sir. Thank you." The young man's tone was dull. He looked straight into the General's eyes.

The older man stared at the wall as silence reigned for a moment. "That will be all for now, Lieutenant. Please inform the other men." He beckoned towards the door.

"Yes, sir." Randon left the room with a heavy spirit. Sorrow dragged his feet slowly across the smooth floor. Pain tugged at his heart, pulling at the threads of hurt and loss.

The General sunk down into his chair, clutching the sides firmly. Grief was written all over his face; each letter shaped like drops of water. "Why? Why did I not bring them all back here? If I had done that, they would still be alive. *His* fiancée would still be living. This is all my fault; I should have thought about an attack." His voice cracked with emotion; the words barely louder than a whisper. His fingers slowly traced a white mark that streaked across his left hand. The scar stretched tight across his skin. *Another scar; another heartless gift from war. But this scar will bleed every day and it will always haunt me.*

The news spread quickly. In the hospital, the nurses were grieving the loss of their companions. Edith was still recovering and lying on one of the cots. Her hair fell in loose curls around her head as she rested against a thin pillow. She'd heard the commotion but hadn't quite realised what everyone was talking about. That is, until one of the other nurses informed her.

The woman was small, with blonde hair pulled back into a bun. Her eyes were friendly, but Edith could tell she held bad news.

"The Germans attacked us back at the barracks. Almost everyone was killed," here she faltered, not wanting to reveal what she knew would hurt the poor girl. "Edith, one of the younger nurses didn't make it."

Edith's expression changed instantly. Concern swept over her face. "Who was it?" she cried.

"Lily. One of the survivors said that Elsie, the oldest nurse, had gone to save her but became trapped in the falling building. Lily was too weak to escape after giving her blood."

Edith could tell by the lady's tone that she was ignorant about *who* the blood had been given to and she couldn't bear to say.

"Oh God, why Lily? *Why*?" She groaned, "She was so young, so innocent. *Why* did she die?" Her heart throbbed; every beat tinged with grief.

The other nurse stood uneasily; not quite sure how to respond. Everyone felt the loss of their friends from that fatal night, but for some, their pain was deeper.

God, help me, please. I don't know what to make of all this. I just want to go home. I can't keep watching all these people die. Please, show me Your will.

She clasped her hands together, squeezing them until her knuckles turned white. Grief and anger wrestled together in her mind.

Lord, I don't understand why you let her die.

She buried her face against the pillow, wetting it with drops of heartache.

The lady silently left the room, disturbed by the scene.

God, I need Denni by my side. I miss him so much.

CHAPTER EIGHTEEN

25 May 1941. It had been three months since Edith's division had retreated back into safer territory, and three months since Lily Porter had died. Her blood had saved Edith's life but ended her own.

Spring was here, slowly bringing beauty to the desolate towns and fields. Flowers peeped above the charred ground, as if too scared to truly open up. Bright green leaves began to decorate the trees that were left, hiding their scarred forms. Birds chirped in the trees, their songs harmonizing together with the sound of crickets and flowing water.

But this beauty was tainted and short-lived. Soldiers still trampled over the ground and tanks crushed anything in their path. Explosions ripped through the land, once again sending it into heaving fits.

§

"Edith, the doctor wants to see you." The young soldier motioned towards her as she sat under the sprawling oak tree. Bright green foliage cast longing looks across the ground, their shadows spreading dark shapes. Sunlight flicked through the branches, showering golden drops of sunshine onto the green leaves.

A small book rested in the folds of her dress. Three months of rest had done her much good. Almost entirely healed from her wound, she was now able to serve her country once again.

She followed the soldier back into the building; a thousand questions permeated her mind. They paused in front of a grey-toned door waiting for someone to answer the young man's firm knock.

"Come in. That will be all, thank you," the doctor directed his speech towards the soldier with a kindly smile. "Now, Edith, I have some news for you. I have received word that our colleagues back in America would like some trained and experienced nurses to join them at Pearl Harbour, a naval base in Hawaii. I've called you here because I know you are highly skilled in what you do, not to mention a very compassionate nurse. You've definitely had plenty of experience in war, and I think you're perfect for this mission. I doubt you'll have much to do at Pearl Harbour. The likelihood of an attack is very slim but still, they would appreciate the service. Do you have any good reason why

I should not send you?" He leaned back into his chair, resting his hands on the smooth wooden sides.

Edith stood silent for a moment. Her face was a mixed expression of excitement and curiosity. "I definitely didn't expect that, sir. I don't have any reason not to, and I would be very glad to assist in any way I can. I do have two questions, though, sir." She waited, expectantly.

He waved her on with a smile.

"Why me? I mean, surely there are plenty of other nurses who are far more skilled than me. And why do they wish to have experienced nurses at Pearl Harbour if there is no risk of attack?" Her eyebrows curved upwards.

"I chose you because I have seen your courage amidst battle, and you are very dedicated to your work. Also, I believe your faith helps you stay hopeful during this time, and that is something we definitely need out here. I don't quite understand why they want the nurses at Pearl Harbour. I think it might be as a backup. You'll need to leave in two weeks."

"Thank you, sir." She stepped towards the door. "Oh, and sir, this mission isn't secret, is it? I wish to tell my fiancé; so he won't be worried about me."

"No, it's not a secret. Thank you for your concerns."

Edith left the room. *God, I know none of this surprises You, but it does me. Help me to trust You. I am willing to go, but it's all new again.*

THE NURSE

CHAPTER NINETEEN

Dearest Edith,

I can't begin to describe how much I miss you. It seems like time itself has paused - and you're so far away. I guess God's helping me to trust in Him because when you were wounded, I spent several days praying and begging that He would let you live. I'm so relieved to hear that you are now, finally, recovered. Remember, Edith, even if you or I are struggling, which I know we both are, God can never be surprised. He's walking us through these trials, and I believe He's helping us grow stronger in Him, and stronger in our love for each other. My father always used to tell me that one of the best ways to know if you truly love a person, is to spend time without them, and see if you miss them. I sure am missing you! God knows how earnestly I look forward to the day that we will be forever joined together by marriage. Stay strong in the Lord, Edith. I am praying for you. I'm glad to hear about your trip to Pearl Harbour. I once was there as a little kid - it's so beautiful, but I wish I was there with you. I must admit, it's a

lot easier for me, knowing that you will be somewhere far safer.
Write to me as soon as you can, darling Edith.
I love you.
Denni

She lifted the letter to her lips, gently kissing the brown faded paper. "I love you, too," she whispered as she slipped it into her luggage. Sunlight peeped through the grey skies as she walked toward the train station with several other soldiers and nurses. Birds sang cheerfully as they rested in the tall, majestic trees.

"All aboard," the station-master shouted. His neatly arranged clothes were symbolic of his character. Small beady eyes peeked from his oddly shaped face, and overgrown stubble framed a peculiar smile. His hair matched the colour of the sky - grey and sober.

The group hurried towards the waiting train, boarding without a word, except for a polite thanks to the man who took their tickets.

"What do you think it will be like?" one of the nurses asked. She was a pretty creature; her dark hair sweeping to the side of her face, and delicate grey eyes that seemed to sparkle even during the hardest of times.

A young soldier was sitting beside her on the hard seat, looking out the window at blurry scenery. "Well, from what I've heard, and I can't say it's much, it would seem it's a very warm and idyllic place. I don't expect we'll have much to do. It'll be more like a holiday." He smiled pleasantly at her, then turned his gaze towards Edith. "Do you have any idea?"

"I've never actually been there myself, but my fiancé has. He said it's very beautiful." She stared out the window, remembering Denni's last letter.

"I didn't know you were engaged, Edith!" The nurse exclaimed, eyes sparkling with delight. "Oh please, let me see your ring."

Edith smiled, holding out her hand to the eager young lady.

"It's pretty." She faltered— "a bit different, but—"

"Mya!" The young soldier shot her a reproving look.

"Oh, it's fine. I don't mind," Edith laughed sweetly, watching the two young people with a warm feeling. "In my opinion, it's the prettiest ring I've ever seen."

"Your fiancé is Denni Alber, isn't he?" the young man asked.

"Yes."

"He is a very brave man. If it wasn't for him, I wouldn't have volunteered. I must admit, he's a bit of an inspiration to me."

"Yes, he's very brave. I miss him so much." She swallowed the lump that had just formed in her throat.

"I hope I can be like him, someday," he murmured.

Edith smiled kindly at the young man. "You've already been very brave."

Outside, the world swept by in a blurred array of verdant fields, princely trees, and simple cottages.

CHAPTER TWENTY

Turquoise waves splashed gently across the shore; white foam dancing across the silvery water. Sand, scorched by the fiery sun, shone in the evening light.

The sky was a painting; red streaks dabbled earth's roof, mixing with slashes of gold that dusted each fluffy cloud. Birds sang a gentle song, each one forming its own part of nature's melody.

Several buildings were nestled near the beach, their brightly painted walls mirroring the scenery around them. Fighter planes slept in tall sheds, their dark sides spreading shadows across the hard floor.

Out in the sparkling water, an array of ships and boats decorated the harbour. Soldiers walked casually among the shady trees, and pleasant chatter hung gently on the sweet-smelling air.

Edith stood on the beach, her bare feet soaking in the warmth of the white sand. Her skirt hung just above her knees and a delicate pink blouse was tucked in. Her complexion was tinted brown by the sun, but her eyes still looked as blue as ever.

"Denni, I wish you were here so we could enjoy this together. I miss you so. You were right - it is gorgeous." She whispered to herself; her voice barely audible.

"Edith, do you mind if I speak to you for a moment?" She turned around, unaware that anyone had been present. Mya stood before her, white teeth glinting in the sun.

"Oh sure, I wasn't really speaking to myself by the way. I was just making a memory."

Mya grinned - "Yes, I guessed."

"Well, how can I help you?"

She twitched uneasily on her toes. "Um, oh...I don't know where to start."

"It's alright, I'm happy to listen."

"Thank you. You remember the young soldier on the train with us?"

Edith nodded, starting to understand where this was heading.

"Well, you see...he proposed to me yesterday. I didn't know what to say...I told him that I would have to think about it. But I feel guilty; like I've done something wrong."

"Do you like him?"

"Yes, I do...he's very caring and sweet and all that, but—" she paused.

"But what?"

"He's not a Christian. My father always told me that I should never allow myself to start liking someone who isn't a Christian. He showed me what the Bible teaches about being equally matched and the importance of being married to a believer. But I'm struggling; I really want to do the right thing, but I do like him."

"Mya, your father is totally right. You can't afford to let yourself have feelings for someone who doesn't share the same faith as you. I'm sure he's very nice; he seemed like an honest young man when I met him, but God does tell us not to marry unbelievers. You really need to pray and ask God for His help in making this decision.

The girl's eyes glistened with tears. "I know you and my father are right, it's just *I so want* to have someone special."

"I was in the exact same situation as you are now. I desperately wanted to have someone beside me during this time, and for the rest of my life. I really had to learn to trust God, and I still struggle being here without Denni. If it's God's will for you to get married one day, He will bring the right man along for you. You've got to keep trusting Him. It's a hard struggle, I know...and I will be praying for you."

" I haven't really had any peace all along, I just didn't want to admit it. I really appreciate you talking to me." Her eyes moistened yet hope shone through.

"So," Edith looked into her eyes with such a gentle

expression that even the wildest temper would have melted. "Will you tell him no?"

Mya sighed, "Yes, I will. But I need to tell him why."

She patted the girl's shoulder comfortingly. "War becomes an excuse for some to forsake God, but we need to cling harder to Him during these times."

"Yes..." Mya smiled as she walked away. Her step was light, and Edith could tell that she had found some peace.

Edith sank down into the sand, soaking up the heat. The sun dipped below the clouds as she sat there, watching the sky darken.

CHAPTER TWENTY-ONE

A young sailor stood on the deck of the *USS Arizona*, watching as the water rippled against the sides of the mighty vessel. His white uniform shone brightly in the morning sun as the wind gently ruffled his dark hair. He took one final look at the resplendent scenery before him, then climbed carefully down into the ship's interior. Inside the sleeping berth, several of his messmates sat around a table, playing with a weather- worn deck of cards.

"What you boys doin'?" He perched on one of the bunks, his legs slightly moving in time to the ship as it rocked gently in the harbour.

"Playing the obvious," one of them replied with a sly laugh. "Wanna join?"

The sailor grinned but shook his head. "I'm fine, thanks... gotta do something." He manoeuvred his way through the rows of tidy bunks until he found his. Hoisting himself up onto the top bed, he lay low, trying to avoid banging his head on the protruding structures above him.

He slipped his hand under the pillow, letting his calloused fingers grasp the small picture. He pulled it out, his eyes running over every detail.

A young woman smiled at him. Dark curly hair and distinct beauty were clearly visible even despite how faded the memory was.

A silent sigh escaped his lips as he once again returned the picture to its home. "Please, wait for me," he whispered.

"Jack, Cap'tain needs you on-board." The sailor sprung up from his resting place, collecting his thoughts.

"Comin, sir," he replied as he hastily left the room.

§

December 6, 1941.

Dear Denni,

Your letter gave me great comfort. I must admit, I am enjoying being at Pearl Harbour, except it's not the same without you. We should come here for our honeymoon. I'm looking forward to another day of rest tomorrow. Some of the girls and I have planned some time at the beach, seeing as there's not much to do. It does make me wonder why we're here.

She paused, a yawn controlling her face for a second. Sleep dragged at her eyes, begging for mercy. "I guess I'll just finish this tomorrow."

She walked over to the bed, which was a much better

affair than her previous one. Her auburn hair was braided and slipped down by the side of her face. Another yawn crept in...closely followed by a second.

§

Dark shadows flew across the rippling water. The dull drone coming from engines hung heavy in the air. A large circle the colour of blood marked the side of every plane. The metal sides of the Japanese Zeros gleamed in the early morning sun.

The fields were beginning to glimmer from drops of dew that moistened their gentle stalks when the shadows crossed over. They headed towards the harbour, where rows of steel-bound ships lay docked, rocking in the tender billows. Several soldiers stood in groups, talking together, and a few marines were busy attending to the needs of these princely rulers of the sea.

The *USS Arizona* stood proudly in the water, her sides gleaming in the light. Over on the shore, the land still rested in a sleepy state. The buildings lay quiet, with only a little movement now and then.

The shadows slipped closer until their figures were clearly outlined by the sun. A few people looked up but didn't take notice. After all, Pearl Harbour was a naval base, and they were accustomed to regular visits from planes.

Then it happened.

THE NURSE

CHAPTER TWENTY-TWO

Out of nowhere, torpedoes, glistening in the light, fell with heavy thuds as they hit their targets. Flames burst into action. Smoke shrouded the water. Screams pierced the air as the once peaceful sea was turned into a churning strip of fire. Soldiers and marines alike dashed into the oily water as flames and bullets devoured their bodies.

The ships creaked and groaned as torpedoes tore through their sides, ripping through the heavy metal and exploding inside the interior.

Aboard the *USS Arizona*, several sailors clambered out of the bunks, covering their ears as the emergency sirens pierced through the air.

Jack stumbled through the doors and lurched towards the deck. His eyes widened in horror as he beheld the sea of fire before him. Black smoke billowed up in deathly plumes. His gaze trailed down to the water below him. Oil bubbled across it in voluminous amounts.

A blood-curdling scream echoed by him as a sailor ran blindly towards the edge of the ship. Flames licked his body as he pushed against the railing.

Jack raced towards him, ignoring the bullets ricocheting all over the deck. Something smashed into his leg, but he pushed on. He grasped the man, wincing as the flames singed his skin, and feebly pushed him overboard. A splash assured him of the man's relative safety.

A Japanese plane flew through the smoke, heading towards the ship. It released a single bomb and sped away. A massive explosion tore through the ammunition hold. The ship split in two as smoke and fire devoured its iron form. In seconds, the *USS Arizona* slipped under the water, carrying with her the lives of over a thousand trapped men.

Jack writhed in the water, gasping for air as the pull from the *Arizona* sucked him down under its massive body. He tried to swim away, but it was too strong.

The oil in the water clouded his sight as he sank down; his lungs filling with liquid. "Emily." The name flashed through his mind one last time.

The dark shadows skimmed through the sky, releasing a torrential downpour of bullets into the masses of helpless men as they slipped and slid in the tipping ships. Bloodied limbs floated in the smoky water, and charred figures sunk or were pulled down by blood-hungry predators lurking amidst the depths.

As the planes reached the end of the harbour, they spun around, and headed back towards the rows of burning ships, once again dropping their fatal iron-clad weapons.

Edith raced around the hospital, screaming for the other nurses. Their faces were white with shock and fear. "Come on, we need to get prepared!" she cried, grabbing handfuls of bandages and several drugs. A loud explosion sounded nearby, and glass shattered across the floor.

"Be careful but go as fast as you can. Come on, the men need us!" she urged as they rushed into action. Several soldiers raced towards the door carrying a mangled form between them.

"Bring him over here."

They laid the screaming man on one of the cots, quickly administering a powerful painkiller with shaking hands. Footsteps thudded as several more severely wounded marines and soldiers were brought in. The floor quickly took on a crimson stain.

The explosions outside were constant. They could hear the planes circling above in the sky, and the heart wrenching screams.

Mya rushed around the building, helping tend to the masses of wounded men that were pouring in. Soldiers with limbs half hanging off limped or crawled towards the hospital doors.

The smell of burnt flesh hung heavy on the air.

"Mya, help me, please," one soldier whispered, trying to catch her attention. A severe burn had left his arm a gruesome mess. Blood stained the rest of his body.

She rushed over, helping him onto the hard cot. Dark smears coloured her uniform, as she was overwhelmed by intense emotion. "Oh, Edmund, please no," she begged as she wiped away the blood with shaky hands.

"Mya," he stared into her eyes, each breath a pang of agony. "I love you."

"Please, don't say anything, just let me help you." She wrapped a cream-coloured bandage around his arm. His pale face screwed up in pain.

"Over here, quick!" Edith's voice urged. She ran towards the door. Planes roared overhead. Every explosion released a tremor that shook the foundations of the building. Black smoke hid the mangled forms of the ships; bright flames hissed as they met water.

Each scream was like an arrow that pierced the souls of every person as they lived out that fatal day. Heart-wrenching and agonizing, they simply spoke of death.

Edith glanced around the building. Blood spattered the white floor as the nurses worked faster than ever. Her attention was caught by the maimed form of a soldier lying in the doorway. His eyes were glazed, and blood plastered his charred and oily face. She ran over and tried to feel his pulse. Nothing.

"Help me move him," she shouted to a soldier who looked as if he was walking whilst sleeping. He jerked to attention.

She noticed a trickle of crimson sliding down his arm, but he seemed to be unaware of it. They gently lifted the body and placed it on a table alongside others.

In a desperate attempt, a few brave pilots risked their lives and headed inside the aircraft sheds. They could feel the earth shake as the bombs smashed into the buildings around them. Struggling to dodge the bullets, they slowly managed to take to the skies, and were pursuing the Japanese Zeros in fierce determination.

Floating bodies and limbs rocked gently in the water and black pools of oily liquid clung to anything in their way. Several of the ships were half capsized, their passengers trapped beneath layers of metal. The screams of those poor men crying out to be rescued would seem to be enough to thaw the hardest of hearts.

But it didn't.

The *Oklahoma* was upside down, water slapping against its great metal sides. The noise of hundreds of men screaming and pounding against the iron haunted the air. Trapped inside the massive ship, their chance of escape was delicately thin. The atmosphere was stuffy inside that metal cage. The smell of tears and perspiration hung heavy in the air.

Above the ship's hull, flames and water fought together in hissing fury. Hundreds of men floated in the water, often knocking into the lifeless forms of their companions and friends. For those still trapped above in the ships, their only route of rescue was jumping into the water.

Many met Death though before they reached the sea; slipping and sliding down the sides of the tipping vessels. Sharp, jagged chunks of metal tore through flesh and bone and blood mingled with the bleak water.

A man lost his grip on the railing of one of the ships to which he had been holding onto in desperation. He fell headlong, striking his head against the tough edge. The sunlight reflected on the metal band around his finger now sparkling red.

Back inside the hospital, casualties and deaths were overwhelming. Piles of bodies, blackened and shredded by the bombs that kept falling upon Pearl Harbour, lay on racks; anywhere to make space for the constant new arrivals.

The screams and groans of those writhing in pain blurred into one monotonous echo around Edith as she numbly administered powerful painkillers and wrapped strips of cloth around relentless wounds.

Several cheers ruptured the noisy air outside as an American plane shot down one of the enemy. It crashed into a field, exploding into a huge burst of fire and smoke.

Slowly, the Japanese Zeros started to leave. Chased by

American fighters, they flew through dusty skies, their shadows floating across the slick blackened waters.

Death rocked gently in the harbour that day as hundreds of men rested in their watery graves.

A few survivors swam numbly among the ships, trying to find a form of safety; away from their dead companions.

A small photograph floated in the water; its sides were singed and stained red. Hands that once so fondly held it now lay lifeless in the depths below.

THE NURSE

CHAPTER TWENTY-THREE

Tap, tap, tap.

The young marine heard faint sounds coming from the *Oklahoma*. He cautiously walked closer to the vessel, turned upside down by the fatal battle earlier that morning. The noise continued but this time it was accompanied by shouting voices. The man dropped to his knees, placing his ear against the metal.

"Help, please...we're trapped!" The men's cries were desperate and heart-breaking.

"Over here, quick! I need your help!" The marine grabbed a hammer, smashing it against the ship's hull. The metal bent slightly, a small dent forming. Several others joined him, and the air soon filled with clanging.

§

Edith sat outside the hospital, head resting in her hands. It had been two days since the attack on Pearl Harbour. Mangled ships still lay resting in the water. She stared numbly at the deathly silent *USS Arizona*. Over a thousand dead men lay trapped in that metal grave.

Oh God, be with those men's families...how will they cope knowing their loved ones are never coming home again? I thought there'd be nothing to do here but I'm exhausted. I was totally unprepared for this. Thank You, God, for keeping me safe. So many people have died, and it could have so easily been me. Why, God, why did they have to die? Why do all those families have to lose the people closest to them?

She closed her eyes, shutting out the painful scenery before her. Footsteps thudded close by. She looked up and saw several soldiers running past. Excitement seemed to have washed away the fear that had only just recently clouded their expressions.

"What is it?" She stood up abruptly.

"America has declared war on Japan. We're going to show them who's in charge," a soldier with ruddy cheeks declared to the startled nurse.

"War?" She raised her eyebrows. "*We're at war now?*"

"Yes, the president announced it just yesterday. Japan caught us by surprise, and we are going to do the same thing back to them. I've heard the general wants to talk to us boys this afternoon." He smiled victoriously.

"What's going to happen here?"

"I don't know...he doesn't think they'll attack us again."

Edith sighed with relief, "please let that be so, Lord."

"Anyway, better be off; gotta spread the word." The group hurried on toward the next building.

Edith sat down, slipped out her diary and gently turned the faded pages until she reached the last entry. She picked up her pen and scratched it against the rough paper.

December 9th, 1941.

It's been two days since Pearl Harbour was attacked. I'm still getting over the shock of the whole thing. Over 2,000 people have died, and I'm sure there will still be many more. Yesterday, the President declared war on Japan. I don't know whether to feel excited or grieved. To be honest, I just want to go home, and never hear about war again. Denni, if you ever read this, then let me tell you something - I love you more than words can express. I can't stop thinking about if I had died one day ago; you know...about us. I am trying to remember, though, that there are no 'what ifs' with God.

She looked up, watching the waves splash along the shore; the normally clear water now riddled with debris that floated atop the murky depths. A blanket of black oil clouded the surface. Birds danced in the gentle breeze, but smoke still shrouded the twisted forms of the torpedoed ships.

Her skirt swished slightly as she rose and headed inside the hospital. Several nurses were attending the wounded patients. Mya stood beside the bedside of one of the invalids. She glanced up as Edith walked towards her.

"Is he alright?"

"Well, the doctor says his wound looks like it will heal; but there is a risk of infection." She stroked the soldier's hand as she wrapped another clean bandage around his arm.

Edith smiled compassionately. "I can see you're struggling with your decision." She looked into the girl's grey eyes; they were watery and full of grief.

"It's so hard *not* to feel any emotion seeing him lying in such pain!" she cried.

"Oh, Mya, I know it is - but you must trust God in this." Edith noticed how damp her own cheeks felt; she couldn't help but remember the day Denni had been brought in, bleeding and unconscious. She sighed. "Think about this, God always has a reason for everything He does. Your example to Edmund during this time may help him realize his need for a Saviour. I'm not saying it will happen, I'm just trying to encourage you."

The girl's eyes brightened slightly. "Thanks. I'm sorry for dumping all my emotions on you. I guess God definitely brought you into my life for a reason. If it wasn't for your godly input, I don't know what I'd be doing now."

"It's God helping you, Mya. But thank you...I do want you to know that I'm always willing to listen and talk."

Edith walked over to the medicine cabinet. She pulled open the glass door and selected a small bottle from the second shelf.

"How are you holding up?" The doctor, a short man with a leader-like countenance, stood next to her. Blood stained his apron and speckled his face.

"Oh hello, Doctor. Excuse me, I didn't see you there." She smiled. "I'm doing okay, thank you. The last few days, I must admit, have been a bit of a struggle."

"Yes, they sure have. I wanted to thank you for your courage and brave example. This war is definitely causing me to rely on God more than ever."

"Yes, I don't think I've ever prayed so much in my life before."

"Well, Edith, remember this; God is in complete control over everything, and we mustn't lose sight of Him amidst all the fear and hurt around us."

"Thank you, Doctor. It's nice knowing I'm not the only believer out here. I was told earlier that the President has declared war on Japan. What will happen to us?"

The wearied man shook his head slowly. "I don't know, Edith. I think some of you will probably be leaving."

He smiled then headed into a small room. She walked back to the rows of beds, gently dosing medicine to each pain-stricken patient.

§

The evening light flickered gently among the tall trees; waves crashed softly against the shore, each splash of water outlined silver by the moon.

Edith sat on a rock that jutted out into the sparkling harbour. Her legs dangled in the cool water. A small brown journal nestled comfortably in the folds of her skirt; her hair was pulled back into a braided twist.

"God," she whispered. "What's going to happen now? Is this all over for me? I do so want to go home to Denni, but I don't want to give up on what needs to be done here. Show me Your will, Lord, please?"

"*Why God, why?* Why have all these people died? What are you doing? If you're in control over everything, *why* are You letting so many die?" She clenched her hand against the grainy rock. She desperately wanted to cry like she'd never cried before, but for some reason the tears just wouldn't come. Her shoulders heaved as she looked out into the water. "I know I've said this so many times before, but I can't keep going on like this...help me, please, Lord. I miss Denni reminding me about Your love, and I need him here by my side. This isn't any place for a girl. Lord, *please*, help me cope," she cried. Her heart felt wrenched in two.

With shaky hands, she slipped open the book before her, tenderly turning the pages. Her fingers stopped at a simple bookmark placed in Proverbs 3.

Here, Edith, take this, and keep it in this chapter. Remember, keep reading God's Word even when you don't feel like it. This chapter is one of my favourites, and it always reminds me of God's faithfulness. The words echoed around her head; she could see Denni's smiling face placing the bookmark in her hands.

She glanced down at the black words...*Trust in the Lord with all your heart, and do not lean on your own understanding. In all your ways acknowledge him, and he will make straight your paths.* Peace flooded her wearied mind.

She closed her eyes. *Lord, I've had it all wrong lately...I've been leaning on my own understanding instead of trusting in Yours. Forgive me, Lord, please...I want to grow closer to You, I want to be directed by You.*

The waves splashed against the shoreline, tugging gently on the tiny grains of sand. Crickets chirped cheerily in the sweet foliage hanging from the tall trees.

THE NURSE

CHAPTER TWENTY-FOUR

Mya sat beside the stiff cot, her Bible laying open in her lap. Deep breathing, every few seconds, was a sure sign of her patient's slumber. *A much-needed rest*, she thought as she fingered through the pages.

Outside, birds sang in harmony, each note a pretty addition to the constant splashing of waves. The sun-kissed sand sparkled like a thousand gemstones. Several soldiers stood talking and others wandered up the balmy shore.

A pause in the rhythmic cycle of breathing caught her attention. Her eyes glanced at the still form. His hair was dishevelled but his face had a look of peace about him.

"Please, even if I never see you again after this is over, please be okay," she whispered.

His eyes flickered open and rested on Mya's face. "You're still here?" He gazed into her eyes.

She nodded slowly. "Edmund, please, while you're resting up, let me read to you?" She held his hand so earnestly it was hard to reject her request.

"Sure" he replied, wincing with pain as he tried to sit up. Gentle hands pushed him back.

"No, stay resting; you're not strong enough." Her voice was soft yet held power over the wounded man.

She sat back in the hard wooden chair and slipped through the pages of her Bible until she reached Romans. Her eyes roamed over the cot; he lay still, looking up at the boring ceiling.

Her lips quivered as she formed the first words in her mind. *God, show him Yourself, please! I know I need to let go, but please, Lord; it's so hard. Help me to be willing to let go.*

The words danced on the air; hope, love, and truth mingling together.

Two hours later, a gentle tap on her shoulder startled the young nurse. She looked around and saw the doctor; his face was so kind, so gentle.

"Mya, the soldiers who were picked to fight are leaving now. Are there any you wish to say goodbye to?"

She shook her head mournfully. "Not really; but I'll go anyway. I think I need to leave this building for a bit."

He smiled understandingly. "I think you should go enjoy the fresh air; go have a walk or rest." His gaze slipped down to the Bible resting on her chair. "Mya, remember, you can't save everyone. But," he added, "you're a brave girl for trying."

She blinked back the tears that were so urgently desiring

to flow. "Thank you, Doctor." She gathered her Bible and walked soberly towards the open doors. The air smelt so sweet; a choir of birds sung their song and below them, the turquoise waves sparkled lazily in the warm sunshine. She knelt and slipped off her shoes. The sand felt so refreshing around her aching feet.

§

The airstrip was dotted with many of the nurses and soldiers she knew. Mingled voices hung in the air; some excited, others regretful. A delicate form stood under a tall tree, watching the procession with mixed feelings. She kept stroking her left hand, now and then lifting it to the sunlight, watching the sun sparkle on the twisted metal ring.

"God, keep the men safe; please, bring them home to their families. Lord, please, end this war," she whispered. *And please take me back to Denni.*

"Time to get going," a loud voice bellowed from inside one of the planes. Emotion overwhelmed many a person that day as they said goodbye to the loved ones they had only recently met. The sun smiled down upon these soldiers' fate as they stepped bravely into the iron birds ready to carry them away to victory or death.

"Goodbye!" Mya waved kindly as the men ascended into the smoky skies. Edith walked over to her.

"I know, it's hard— " she began, but Mya stopped her with a little hand gesture.

"Don't worry, Edith, please. Edmund hasn't gone, he's still here, recovering. I was reading scripture to him earlier; he didn't seem to mind. Oh, how I do wish that he too would come to know Christ. I'm trying to lean on God, and I know that I will never marry him unless he does change. God has been showing me in His Word things I never used to see or believe. I feel as if this war has pulled me closer to Him and is helping me more than ever before."

Edith stood dazzled for a second. "Mya…that is excellent. I am praying for you, and for Edmund. Even if he doesn't change, your time hasn't been wasted; I do hope he does though, for your sake, but well done for trusting God in this."

"You never seem to struggle out here. Why?"

"Oh dear, Mya… I do struggle a lot. If you ever read my diary, you'd see a lot of fears, worries, and things I have been having to deal with lately. Just last night, I was crying out to God, angry that He was letting so many people die. I just try not to express my emotions to other people too much because it's not going to help anybody if I'm complaining. Just like you, I'm learning to trust Him always, and not just when I want to."

"I can't help but think about everyone who has lost a loved one during this war. I haven't been hurt like that.

Have you lost anyone, Edith?"

She was silent for a moment.

"You don't need to tell me, if it hurts you so."

"No, it's fine...I just still miss him so much. He died last year, in France. Killed by a sniper, they say. I was told he died instantly, but I don't think he did. I met a soldier who was fighting beside him; he was wounded, and my brother tried to help him. That's when my brother was killed. I had never been able to say goodbye to him—it's one of the biggest regrets of my life. He was the only sibling I had." She said, her voice faltering. "He went and fought before we were even part of the war because he had been studying at a college in England - and he felt it his duty to help his friends."

"I'm so sorry; I never knew. How awful! I've been so concerned about my own life, and here you are, serving so sacrificially, when you've lost someone so dear to you. How selfish of me!"

"Oh no...don't talk about yourself like that. You've been putting your own life in danger by caring for these wounded men."

Mya nodded numbly. "I guess so."

"Come on, let's go see what needs to be done," Edith smiled softly. *God, please help Mya...and me.*

THE NURSE

CHAPTER TWENTY-FIVE

"Edith, the doctor wants to see you," the medic's voice echoed down the hallway. Back inside her dormitory, Edith stood beside the window, watching the gorgeous scenery around them.

"I wonder why," one of the other girls commented in a curious tone as Edith left the room.

Five minutes later, she stood in front of the doctor, in a small room adjacent to the main hospital building. He stood, trying to smile, but finding it rather difficult.

"Ah, Edith, there you are. I've just received word from my superior; a matter regarding you."

Her eyebrows shot up. "Me? Oh no, Sir, have I done something wrong?"

"No, no, quite the opposite. I've been asked to recommend one of my lieutenant nurses to accompany the critically injured men back to San Francisco. I've chosen you because you have a lot of experience and," he smiled kindly, "I know how much you would like to go home."

She looked at him in amazement. "Me? You mean…"

"Yes, I mean you're going home…I can't say that I won't miss your cheeriness and willingness to serve, but all that said, I'm glad for you. You've been such a brave and dedicated nurse, you deserve this. After you arrive in San Francisco, you'll be helping to train new trainees. Your aid will be very much appreciated considering the immense experience you have in nursing on the front-line."

Her eyes flickered back and forth. "Sir, doctor, I don't know quite what to say…I didn't think, I mean, I didn't expect—" she hesitated, trying to form a polite sentence in her joyous mind. "Thank you, sir."

"You're welcome. I'm sure your man will be relieved to hear you're coming home." His grey eyes smiled warmly at her, but Edith could see the pain behind them.

"When do I leave, sir?"

"Tomorrow. I hope that works for you."

"Yes, thank you, doctor. I have enjoyed working alongside you and thank you for encouraging me spiritually. That's something I've really missed since Denni left."

"It's easy to go astray when you're surrounded by temptation. It's been encouraging to watch you obeying the Lord."

"Well, I try, but it sure is a struggle. Thank you, doctor."

"Now go, enjoy one last day before you leave; that is,

hoping we're not attacked anymore." His smile faded. It was obvious he was remembering that dreadful day.

Edith noticed the changed expression. "Respectfully, sir, I want to help until I leave. Some of the girls here might not see their loved ones for many more months, even years. Let them rest, and I'll take their place."

"Ah, Edith, you are a good girl. Thank you." His countenance brightened a little.

She turned around gently and left the room. It was hard to not feel excited knowing she would see Denni again soon. But she was leaving danger, and others would still be here, braving the odds, not knowing what moment would be their last. *I'll be helping back at home though*, she said to comfort herself.

A sensational thrill sent tingles up her spine. "Denni, I can't wait to see you," she whispered in joyful anticipation.

"Pardon?" The voice caught her off guard. She spun round and came face to face with Mya.

"Oh Mya, whatever is the matter? Are you hurt?"

"Oh no, it's not that; I'm just glad."

"But you're weeping?" Edith's mind was more than puzzled by now.

"I'm weeping because I'm happy."

"Please, you're killing me with curiosity?"

"Edmund is reading my Bible."

"Oh!"

"Yes, he said he'd been half listening to me when I read it to him the other day and that it really impacted him when he heard about the Cross and what Jesus did for him. This morning, he asked if he could borrow my Bible. Oh Edith, could this really be happening?" A smile crept up the corners of her mouth.

"Mya," she stuttered, "I don't know what to say. I mean, that is so wonderful. I'm so glad for you. I hope God is working on his heart. There is so much in God's Word that will show him his need to repent of his sins and trust in Christ alone for salvation. I'll continue to pray for the both of you."

"Thank you. You're so kind!" A confused look took over her face. "What were you saying as I walked up, if you don't mind me asking?"

"Oh—" Edith paused; she struggled knowing that this young woman would be staying in danger to help others. "I was saying that I couldn't wait to see Denni; I know, it's weird that I speak out loud to myself."

"But why were you saying that now?"

"Um—because the doctor told me today that he's chosen me to accompany the critically injured soldiers back to San Francisco. I didn't ask, he just said. I don't want you to think that I am trying to escape all this danger."

"Edith, that's great news! You must be so excited. And I

wouldn't think that! You have always been so brave during the war. Plus, even if you had asked to leave, no one would blame you." She looked into Edith's eyes, trying to assure her.

"Thanks. I hope the same thing happens to you."

"Well, don't worry about me. As you've been so kindly reminding me, I need to be trusting in God, and not on my own understanding. It's a good idea."

"Well, yes, you are right. I just can't help but feel slightly guilty. You all will still be here doing who knows what, and I'll be relaxing—"

"Oh shoosh! We'll be fine. You deserve this. Stop fretting about it and actually let yourself look forward to going home."

"I guess so," she replied. "Thanks. I'll miss talking with you."

"And I you. You've kept me from doing a lot of things even though my friends are doing them. I'll struggle not being able to share my feelings and battles with you."

"Mya, it's God who's stopped you from doing those things, not me. Why don't you pray and share those thoughts with Him? He's always ready to listen."

A spark of hope shot across her face. "Yes, I'll do that. Thanks for always helping me focus on God."

Edith just smiled. "Now, go and relax. I have some work to do."

THE NURSE

CHAPTER TWENTY-SIX

That evening, Edith sat on the familiar rock, her Bible once again in her lap. Her pale pink skirt was slightly wet from the gentle waves that splashed against the shore. Stars twinkled above in a canopy of flickering light. Dancing shadows cast longing looks across the sandy beach.

She picked up the pen and let the ink drip onto the paper.

December 10, 1941. Pearl Harbour.
Today I found out that I am finally going home to Denni. I don't quite know what to think; I'm so excited but I'm struggling with how much easier it will be for me compared to the others. How should I act when I know that I'm returning to safety and many others are not? At least I'll still be helping by training the new nurses. It's my last night here at Pearl Harbour. I'm going to miss this place…it's so gorgeous. I almost feel like it's become a sort of home for me. I'm praying for Mya; she so desperately wants Edmund to come to know

God. I do wonder what will come of it all. I cannot wait to see Denni again; and one day soon become his wife.

She leaned back on her resting place, soaking in the imagery before her. Her ring sparkled in the moonlight that splashed across the water.

There he knelt, holding out the symbol of his love for her. The way he looked into her eyes as he slipped it over her finger. The gentle "I love you" he whispered into her ear.

"Soon, Denni, soon."

§

The morning sun flickered through the leaves, showering the tall trees. Out in the harbour, the water sparkled, gleaming in the rays of light descending into its cool depths. Several people stood together on the dock. The captain and two other marines were busy loading bags onto the ship's deck. Several soldiers were walking towards them, a few stretchers in their midst. Groaning forms lay on the litters.

Edith walked over towards the ship, carrying a small bag in one hand. Mya soon accompanied her.

"Edith, I'll miss you a lot. But I'm so pleased for you. Do write to me and tell me how things are back at home. I do long to know."

"I will. And you must write to me, and tell me how

Edmund is doing, and yourself of course. I won't stop praying for him. Do you know when he'll be sent home?"

"No, I don't. The doctor said that he would be prioritizing sending home all the men whose wounds are life-threatening; and seeing as Edmund's isn't, I guess he'll be staying here for the time being. I think Edmund's hoping that his arm heals up completely so he can serve again."

"I hope he does recover fully. Well, I'm glad that gives you both more time to talk things over."

As they stood on the gangway, Edith took one last look back, her eyes lingering on the buildings and beach that had been her home for the last few months. "It seems so strange to think that four days ago, this harbour was full of ships on fire, and the water filled with dying men."

Mya sighed. "Yes, I know. The ships still look the same though, but they're just skeletons of what they were before.

"You're right."

"Edith, we're going now," the captain called out cheerily.

She turned back round to Mya. "Oh, I will miss you. Stay safe...and keep trusting God." She threw her arms around the girl, trying to hide her tears. Mya was just as affectionate.

"I'll miss you too," she cried. "Do enjoy yourself though; forget the worries here." Her voice was shaky, but Edith knew she meant it.

"I won't forget you. I will enjoy being back at home, but I'll still remember you." She patted the girl's back reassuringly.

"Come on, you need to go," Mya wiped her eyes, and put on a brave tone.

"Thank you. God be with you," she replied, stepping onto the ship. She stood on the deck, allowing herself the view of Pearl Harbour. She could see Mya standing there, waving and smiling amongst the crowd.

The cool breeze rustled her hair as the ship began to move, slowly pushing through the blue water. Edith leaned against the white rail, waving back to Mya. Picking up speed, the long vessel strode through the sea; the golden sun bouncing glorious light across its metal sides. The stretch of water glistened, displaying a perfect shadow dipping into the refreshing expanse. In the distance, the trees swayed in the gentle breeze; she could almost imagine hearing the songs of the birds as they played, dancing in the wind.

Be with them, God, and please, bring them all home safely. She watched as Pearl Harbour slowly slipped out of view. The place she had grown so accustomed to was now fading out of sight. The horrors of war were disappearing beyond the horizon; a mist of fluffy clouds and blue skies were the only thing visible now. But she'd still remember everything so vividly; it's always hard to ignore a nightmare that seems so like reality. And for Edith, that had been her reality for the past two years.

She could still see the boy who had died in her arms. His pale face marred by war. The rows of bodies piling up in a bloodied mess after Pearl Harbour was attacked. The feeling of not knowing if that was her last moment alive. That was yesterday's nightmare.

"I'm going home," she whispered. *I'm actually going home?* Her mind was bewildered with the realization that she was going home for the first time since this war had started. It seemed a dream too good to be true.

Then she remembered Mya. Her last wave as the ship steered out of the harbour. Her willingness to talk to her about her struggles and fears. Her love for Edmund.

She pulled out her diary with the same old pen that had told of so much hurt, death, and pain these last couple of years.

Dear Denni,

I've never done this before in my diary; but today I want to write a note just to you. I'm sitting on the deck of the ship that is finally taking me back home, to you. Words can't describe what my feelings are at the moment. In several days, I'll be with you. And in a few months, I'll be your wife. I wanted to take the time to write out a few promises that I have made to you before we are married.

Denni, I promise to always be your wife. I will love you with all my heart, and all my being. I will submit to you and be willing to lay down my thoughts and desires so that I am able to effectively serve and help you as the Lord allows. I will try to be your helper and be willing to aid you in any task you need me for. I promise, Denni, to love you until my last breath.

She put down the pen and looked at the glistening water. "And that is a promise I will always keep."

She couldn't help but notice a few of the other passengers staring at her. Confused looks cloaked their faces.

Mental note to self; don't keep talking to myself out loud.

"Oh, sorry, was I being a distraction? It's a little habit of mine; I'm trying to stop it." Her smile was rather comical.

A nurse sitting opposite her twitched with a slight laugh. "Don't mind us; I believe we were just wondering what you were doing."

Edith's eyes sparkled; her heart fluttered with excitement.

"Are you going back home?" The nurse smiled warmly at her, glancing around at the other members.

"Yes, I certainly am, to help train new nurses."

"And is someone special waiting for you there?"

Edith looked down at the ring on her left hand and smiled. "My fiancé is there; he was wounded and discharged from my previous location and has been waiting for me."

"How sweet! I wish you all the best."

"Thank you. And do you have someone at home?"

The nurse smiled warmly and pointed towards a dainty necklace around her neck. On the chain, there hung a small locket. "I have two children, all grown up now, and my husband. He couldn't come because he wasn't fit for service. He supported me in going to Pearl Harbour. We both agreed it was the safest place. Turns out, it wasn't though."

"That must have been so hard for you."

"It was, but I felt I owed it to my country. I can't wait to see them all. War teaches us some lessons, that's for...sure," her voice wavered.

"Well, I met my fiancé back in France. When he was wounded, we both struggled with the separation. I still feel like I'm in a dream of sorts. It doesn't feel real that I'm on my way back to see him after so many lonesome months."

"I'm sure he'll be very glad to see you." She smiled.

"I'm not sure if he even knows yet; I wrote him a letter, but I think we'll probably get there sooner," she paused, pondering how Denni would react. "Do you ever feel guilty about leaving the danger?"

"I did at first, but then I remember that I have helped already, and that I didn't ask to leave. It's not like we're running away from danger. And we're still serving our country back at home."

"I'm still trying to tell myself that." She smiled then turned back to look out at the water. Before them was a sea of sparkling blue now and then dappled by snow-white clouds, and beyond that, was a memory that was about to become real again.

CHAPTER TWENTY-SEVEN

The ship rocked to and fro in the billowing waves. Overhead, thunder cracked, and lightning sent flickering shadows across the churning water. In the sick berth, Edith stood beside the bed of one of the wounded patients. His face was a sickly mess; blisters scarred the skin and a bandage was wrapped around both eyes. A deep groan erupted from his hoarse lungs.

She gently wiped a damp cloth across his forehead, speaking in soothing tones. "It's alright, just relax. You'll be home soon."

And so will I.

His face screwed up in pain.

He'll be needing intense care, that's for sure. She carefully removed the bandage around his eyes and surveyed the wound. Dried blood crusted the deep gash, and the burnt skin looked ugly.

She picked up a clean bandage and moistened it slightly. Then, she slowly wrapped it around his forehead. "There you go," she whispered, squeezing his hand reassuringly.

"I'm going up on deck for a few minutes to get some fresh air," she called to one of the other nurses who sat beside a man, or rather, what was left of him. Both legs were stumps, wrapped in bloodied cloth. The woman nodded kindly.

The cold air was an adjustment as she walked up the stairs. Waves slapped against the metal sides and the sky kept rumbling, flashes of light evidence of the storm. Rain pelted down, stinging her face and hands. She found some cover and stood breathing in the fresh air.

A sharp shriek ruptured through the air. Edith's eyes flitted around the ship. It was the same shriek she'd heard back at Pearl Harbour. She rushed down the steps and headed towards the sick berth. Another nurse met her there, worry lines stretched across her face.

"What's the matter?" Edith's eyes searched the sick berth, resting on the shaking bed in the opposite corner.

"It's one of the soldiers. He's experiencing shell-shock." Another agonising shriek pierced the air.

Edith rushed over to the bedside, trying to hold the man's hand. He writhed all over the bed. Sweat was breaking out in beads across his forehead. His eyes were glazed over in fear.

"Get down, get down," he shrieked, trying to escape.

'They're coming. Look, the planes!" The nightmare

was real in his mind. His hands clenched the weapon he thought he held.

"Quick, over here. Someone, help me hold him down," She yelled. A young marine raced over, placing weather-worn arms around the shaking form.

"Let go of me, I need to escape! Help me, I'm sinking!" The man's body throbbed with violent movements. His breathing was rapid, and confusion and fear glazed his watery eyes.

"Calm down, calm down!" She tried soothing him but to no avail.

"I'm on fire!" he screamed; his actions uncontrollable. His broken form jerked and twisted on the bed.

"It's alright, you're safe." Her tone was kind and caring, but she knew that he'd never be able to be safe from his nightmares. An unwanted gift from war - one that would never leave.

His sharp breathing slowly calmed, and sleep temporarily rescued the poor man from his terror.

'Thank you," she whispered to the marine. He nodded but didn't make any sound.

"Are you ok?" she gently asked, searching the young man's eyes; his pupils trembled with fear.

When he finally spoke, the words came slowly. "I just can't help remembering that day." Sorrow choked his words, pulling on them, drowning them in a sea of pain and hurt that could never truly be buried. War scarred people forever.

She didn't know what to say but somehow, the absence of an answer seemed to comfort him more. She closed her eyes for a moment, breathing in the stuffy air. It didn't take long for the memories to drift into her mind.

CHAPTER TWENTY-EIGHT

The sun slowly crept above the grey clouds that pocketed the sky. Soft rays of golden light dusted the blue water; each wave a sparkling billow that rolled gently in the harbour.

The tall form of a battleship strode through the water towards the magnificent bridge that stretched across the expanse. Known for its beauty and design, the Golden Gate Bridge was a pleasant yet haunting sight to the many invalids and wounded men returning home.

Edith stood on the deck, watching as San Francisco came into sight. "Thank you, Lord," she whispered.

Groups of people stood near the harbour, each face telling a different story: mothers waiting to see their sons, unaware of the impact of their injuries; wives searching, trying to catch a glimpse of their loved ones; others, clad in khaki uniforms, watched the ship pull through the water, knowing that they would shortly be embarking on a journey that would lead them into the nightmare these people were returning from.

Voices danced upon the crisp breeze; each note a tale of sorrow, hope, regret, joy, and excitement. Edith went below deck with a torn heart. It was hard to be so close to where Denni was yet at the same time, she felt so far away.

Several soldiers sat on hard benches in the ship's hull. They were all bearing gifts War had bestowed upon them: some missing limbs and others hardly recognizable. Fire had also taken its toll, clothing them in a scarred array of charred flesh and blistered skin.

"Are we in the harbour now?" A war-clad soldier motioned towards her. His right arm was wrapped in a bandage. Only one eye watched her face for an answer. A small locket hung around his neck; the chain was faded but its importance to this man was obvious.

"Yes, we are. We'll be getting off soon, I think." She smiled distantly.

Loud shouts and cries rang through the ship as it docked. She ran up on deck and looked out at the scene before her. Weeping mothers and heart-broken wives stood with glazed expressions. Earnest and hopeful loved ones watched the vessel, waiting, searching, for the heroes they had once known so well. Now everything was different.

You can never truly understand what we've been through, what we've seen. Edith's heart raced as she scanned the groups of people. There was only one face her eyes were seeking.

But she couldn't see it.

He wouldn't know yet.

She tried to console herself.

Someone nudged past her. She spun around, locking eyes with the soldier from down below. Her eyes rested on his locket, or rather, where it had been before. "Where is it?" she asked, a concerned expression scrawled across her face.

He looked down and grief swept over his eyes. His hands stumbled around his pockets and then back to his neck. "I don't know," he stuttered, rushing back down the stairs.

Edith watched him with sorrow. The simplest things were sometimes the most special and loved during War. The warm breeze rustled her hair as she stepped off the ship. She stuck close by as the wounded were carefully carried off the vessel.

Gasps and haunted faces met the soldiers as they walked on with the stretchers. Looks of horror cloaked the countenance of many a person that day as they beheld the ones who had recently been fighting the desperate battle for their freedom.

How will they understand? Questions clouded her mind like the clouds covering the soft-blue sky.

They headed towards the hospital trucks that stood waiting. "Where are they taking them?" Edith asked an aged lady clothed in a clean nurse's uniform.

"To a hospital, dearie." She smiled kindly yet the tone of her voice was condescending.

Do I really look stupid to you? Edith thought. Frustration boiled up inside her. *Lord, help me to stay patient.*

"Thanks - I know they're going to a hospital, but would you mind telling me which one, please?" She tried hard to speak kindly.

The lady glanced at her; curiosity written all over her ancient face. She sighed heavily. Then something caught her eye and her expression changed instantly. "Dear me, I'm sorry if I wasn't any help. You're one of the front-line nurses, aren't you?"

Edith smiled subconsciously—"Yes. I've come back to help train the new nurses. I know the men on that ship, so please, if you have any information of where they are going, I would love to know."

"Thank you, dearie, for your service. I've heard lots of horrid things about the war across the sea. You've all done us proud. I believe they're being taken to the army hospital just across town. If you ask around, I'm sure someone could take you." She shook her head sadly.

Edith nodded gratefully. "Yes, it was awful. Thank you." She turned around and headed towards a small building. A white-washed sign hung above the door, reading: *Cafe on The Bay*. Inside the room, several tables, stained a dark red, covered the floor and were occupied by a variety of people. A few soldiers stood in the corner, talking in hushed tones. Edith walked up to the counter and smiled kindly at the young woman who was serving the drinks.

"Hello, miss, what I can get for you today? Nurses and soldiers dine free by the way." Her youthful smile tugged at Edith's heart - *I feel like I've grown up so much since the beginning of this war.*

"Thank you. Just a cup of coffee, please."

"Right away, miss. Were you on the ship that brought home the wounded soldiers this morning?" The girl chatted as she prepared the drink.

"Yes, I was." Edith tried to shake her eyelids open, wary of the sleep that was trying to conquer her.

"What is it like, I mean, over there?"

"It's like living in a constant nightmare. You're trying to save your own life and everyone else's with death all around you."

The girl's eyes widened with horror—"How did you cope?"

"I wouldn't have managed if it wasn't for God."

"Well, I'm glad that we both have something to keep us hoping during this war."

Edith smiled as she recognized the similar faith in this girl; a faith like her own. She gratefully took the steaming cup of coffee and tried to persuade the young waitress to accept the note she held in her spare hand.

Smiling, she replied, "No, please. I told you; nurses and soldiers dine free. It's a small gift in return for your sacrifice but thank you."

Edith thanked the girl again, then made her way towards a small table in the corner of the building.

She sighed in relief as she sat down; *I'm glad I can be by myself.* Steam spiralled up in curling wisps from the cup before her.

Just like the smoke at Pearl Harbour.

She took a deep sip, letting the hot liquid flow down her dry throat. It almost hurt but she didn't think about it.

She let her eyes close. Fatigue was too strong for her to keep fighting back against the sleep that tugged at her weary eyelids.

"Over here; quick. We need a nurse!" The soldiers were yelling. She could see the body lying on the ground. The face was so young. So innocent. And so maimed. Something felt hot and sticky against her skin. She looked down; the boy lay in her arms. His blood staining her uniform. "Please...don't...let...me...die," he begged through bloodied lips. Then his body went limp; his hand still holding hers.

Edith's eyes jerked open.

I guess sleep did get the better of me.

She picked up the cup from the table.

Cold coffee.

Oh God, will I always have these nightmares? Will I always remember everything I saw?

THE NURSE

CHAPTER TWENTY-NINE

Edith stood in a large room; its walls polished white. Several young women sat on benches before her, their bright young faces a mask of ignorance. They all wore nurses' uniforms. Carefree countenances plastered their features.

Edith inhaled deeply: *Lord, help me word this right.*

"My name is Edith; I've been serving overseas for the last few years now. After the attack on Pearl Harbour, I was asked to come train you all. Hopefully, my experiences from the war will help me prepare you for service. But first, I want you to understand something. War is never pleasant. I've seen things I never wished to see. I've seen limbs hanging off, skin shredded in bloodied ribbons. I've seen men walk right into the face of danger, to protect their country, and I've also seen the same men shaking with fear so strong they can't control it. I've seen bodies mutilated and half eaten by rodents. I've held boys in my arms who were no older than you as they writhe and convulse because of the agony searing through their body. I've watched them die and I've heard them whisper their last words to me. For hours upon hours, I've smelt the stench of burning flesh and I've heard the screams of men as they die; screams that cause your blood to curdle. And I can tell you one thing for sure; I hate war. There's nothing romantic about it! It destroys your emotions, and it destroys you, mentally and physically. You need to go overseas with the view that you're fighting for your life! Because I'm telling you, if you're not prepared beforehand, you won't survive out there. These men need heroes not cowards!"

But it's so hard to willingly become a hero when almost certain death is all you get.

She swallowed hard, trying to ignore the memories that were so vividly repainting themselves before her mind.

A strange smell wafted through the air. It was a burning odour that brought the past back to her mind.

Her eyes flitted around the room.

A soldier was there, his arm engulfed in flames.

She quickly stepped forward, moving towards the apparent man.

His blood-stained eyes were glazed over, his face a blank picture.

Her hands fumbled around on the floor, trying to find the figure of the man in her head.

Deep wheezing echoed by her.

"Where is he?"

*The burning smell was heavy on the air. It smelt like...*she looked down at the ground and sighed...*Pearl Harbour.*

It was haunting.

"Excuse me," a slight tap startled her. She spun around and locked eyes with one of the young trainees who stood before her. The others were still seated, bewildered looks blanketing their faces.

One of the older girls motioned gently towards the door, the soft smile on her face somehow conveying that she understood Edith's need for a moment of peace. The rest quietly walked out in single file, the odd few casting inquisitive glances as they left the room.

"Yes?"

"Are you alright?" The girl's eyes were a mirror of concern.

The smell: it was right here.

Her gaze followed along the room and towards the window. Smoke fogged the air outside.

It was that smell; it was bringing back memories.

"What's happening out there?" She gasped.

"There was an oil spill, but it's under control now." The girl explained.

"Oh, have I been acting strange?"

The girl's face said it all.

"Oh dear, it's just, that smell reminded me of Pearl Harbour."

A look of sober understanding clouded her features. "So, it is true," she whispered.

"What's true?"

"The stories about the nightmares. My dad served in the Great War; I never knew him, but my mum said he came back a different man. She hardly recognized him. Every night, he'd wake up screaming and writhing around, reliving the horrors he had witnessed for so long. Over time, he became crazier and then it happened." Her eyes were filling with drops that only sorrow can produce.

"What happened?"

"One night, his nightmares were worse than usual. He thought my mum was the enemy. He tried to attack her; she was so scared that she pushed him back and he hit his head against the table. The injury killed him. My mum has always felt so burdened by guilt; she thinks it's her fault. I don't want to turn out like that."

Edith looked into the girl's face; the pain and fear were so clear behind those sea-blue eyes. "War is so hard. I lost my brother a couple years ago. He died in action, and I never got to say goodbye. I don't quite know how to help you, but all I can say is you've got to just keep hoping; hoping in the Lord that He'll end this war."

"Do you think I should go?"

A deep sigh erupted from her lips. "Yes, I think you should. As you heard me say before, there is nothing sweet over there, apart from the knowledge that the men who've died aren't suffering anymore. But we need people like you; the men need help. Go, and do whatever you can to help your country."

"I will." The girl dashed her hand across her eyes. She turned around, heading towards the entrance. As a second thought, she spun around and ran back to Edith. She gave her a quick hug, whispering "thank you."

Edith tried to fight back the lump forming in her throat. "You're welcome."

THE NURSE

CHAPTER THIRTY

"Careful, make sure you're not pushing it in too hard," Edith gently reminded the young trainee as she practised with the needles.

The girl nodded slightly and attempted the same procedure for the tenth time on the manikin. She released a short sigh. "When will I get it right?"

"It's okay," Edith encouraged. "It took me a while, too." She smiled kindly at the girl. *God, please end this war before so many more young people have to die.*

"Excuse me, Edith, the doctor wants to see you." Another young nurse stood waiting at the door, beckoning towards her.

Edith walked over and headed in the direction given to her by the girl. After walking several steps down a crisp-white hallway, she reached a small room marked "office".

She tapped once on the door.

"Come in, please."

She stepped in. "Thank you, sir."

The doctor was a tall, sober-faced man with twinkling brown eyes. He stood up politely as she approached, gesturing towards a chair in front of his cluttered desk. "Now, miss Edith, seeing as you only arrived here three days ago, I expect you must still be recovering from your time at Pearl Harbour. You must be very tired indeed. Where have you been staying these last two nights, if you mind me enquiring?"

Edith smiled briefly. "Yes, you're right. I do feel very tired. I've been staying at the hotel over the road."

He nodded. "Ah, that one...do you have any relatives or family nearby?"

"Yes, I have an aunt who lives in the countryside and my fiancé does too."

"In that case, then, I'm giving you a five-day break. Go and see your family and rest. We will need all the help we can get from you afterwards, but I want to ensure that you have had time to regain your energy. I can't begin to imagine what you must be feeling after going through such an awful experience like Pearl Harbour."

Edith cringed at the thought. "Thank you, sir. I do appreciate it."

"No, it is I who appreciates everything *you* have done."

She smiled and left the room.

§

The wind blew gently against Edith's legs as she stepped off the train. Everything looked so familiar, yet also so strange. Puffy white clouds hung low in the sky and the constant chirping of crickets was a pleasant reminder that she was home.

She gathered up her bags and headed inside the station. The cooler air was refreshing to her face. Inside the building, soldiers, nurses, and civilians mingled alike. Signs decorated the walls, each trying to encourage young men and women to join up and serve their country.

That was me a few years ago, she thought, watching a young woman who was intently studying the sign. *It was so easy then, but now?*

"Edith, is that you, Edith?" A confused voice broke through her thoughts. The accent was familiar, a tugging reminder of her home. She spun around and saw an old man dressed in a station-master uniform. Time was stretched across his face in weary lines. Grey stubble covered his chin, matching the sparsely placed hair upon his head.

"Mr. Dandon? I didn't realise...oh—" Her sentence was cut short as the old man enveloped her in a friendly hug.

"You survived the war?" His breath came in short gasps.

"Yes...I didn't know you worked here or lived here, to say the least. Last time I saw you, I was helping you in that cafe of yours."

"I know, dear girl...I moved here a few years ago after my wife died. Our son offered me a place to stay, and I was glad to be with his family. I needed to earn more. I was too old to enlist so I help out here a few days of the week. It's not much, but it helps."

"I'm so sorry about your wife; she was always so friendly. I'm glad though, that you have managed to find a job."

"Now, let me look at you. You haven't changed a bit. I'm sure you are the wiser, but you still look as young as ever."

Edith smiled warmly; she hadn't expected to see Mr. Dandon here.

"Oh Edith, I heard about your brother. Such a sweet young man." He looked into her eyes with such a tender expression.

"Thank you. I miss him every day of my life." She swallowed hard. "I need to get going, now. I have someone I'm waiting to see."

"Goodbye, Edith. I'm so glad you're back and safe."

She walked out of the train station and stood for a moment in the gentle breeze. Rolling hills cast shadows across the wheat-coloured grass. The song of birds was a sweet melody dancing in the wind.

She headed towards a row of vehicles waiting for passengers.

"Do you need a ride, miss?" The short driver opened the

cab door and gestured towards it.

"Yes, thanks." She climbed inside. The leather seats felt so comfortable. *Denni, I'm almost here.*

"Here is the address," she said, passing a small slip of paper to the man. The engine started; and she began her last journey home.

§

Inside a small, white, rustic house, Denni sat on a comfortable chair; a worn book resting in his hands. A light knock at the door interrupted his silent musings. He stiffly stood and hobbled over. With one hand, he opened it; the other leaning against the frame for support.

Sunlight flickered in, dazzling his eyes for a moment.

Then he saw *her*.

Standing so perfectly in the light; auburn hair dancing in the wind. Her face was as gorgeous as ever. Those blue eyes sparkling in the light.

"*Edith*!" he gasped. 'Oh, *is that really you?*" Tears filled his eyes, blurring his vision as she stepped towards him. Her arms wrapped around him.

"Oh, Denni...I've missed you an awful lot," she cried, burying her face into his willing shoulder.

"You're actually here? *Please*, tell me it's real...*let it not be a dream?*" He gently lifted her head, staring deep into her eyes.

"Yes, *I'm truly here*," she whispered—"with you. *I'm home now*."

He couldn't speak. He just stared so tenderly at her; his heart bursting with love and relief. "Oh, you don't know how much I've worried about you. And to have you home, now, finally, after all these months? *I love you*." He pulled her close, kissing her hair so affectionately.

"I love you, too," she cried. "Did...did you get my letter? The one saying about me coming home?"

"No, I think the post has been delayed. But that doesn't matter now. *My darling, you're home now*," he whispered into her ear.

The sun shone down upon the two as they stood there, tears flowing freely, hearts throbbing and mending at the same time.

As dusk took control of the sky, shedding eerie yet beautiful glows across the land, Edith left the small house.

Denni stood by the door, leaning against the post. "I love you," he called out to her as she headed down the track towards her aunt's house.

She glanced back, the soft glow from the moon outlining her delicate figure. "And I you," she replied tenderly, stroking the band of commitment and love around her finger.

CHAPTER THIRTY-ONE

Edith wrapped her knuckles gently across the door, and then stood waiting. The wind whistled through the streets, sweetly beckoning the leaves to join in an autumnal dance.

"Hello, please come in." A woman stood in the doorway, a pleasant expression masking her face, and yet, Edith could see the heartache in her eyes.

"Thank you. I'm sorry to interrupt you." She followed the woman inside. They walked through into a large room, elegantly furnished. Edith caught her breath; but it wasn't the finery that caught her attention.

In the corner, resting gently on a mahogany dresser, stood an oval picture frame. A girl's face was enclosed in it, the sides of the picture slightly faded.

The lady watched Edith, noticing her keen interest. A sad smile creased her lips as she picked up the frame, holding it ever so gently. "This was our daughter. She was such a pretty girl." The woman paused for a moment, and then looked straight into Edith's eyes. They glistened in the soft light. "Did you know her?"

"Yes...that's why I'm here."

§

"I met her when I was serving over in France, as a nurse. Despite her age, she was one of the bravest nurses I've ever met. During one of the battles, I was wounded. The doctor said I needed a blood transfusion, but it was hard finding a donor. That was when Lily offered to give hers. I was unconscious at that time, but another nurse told me later about what she had done. Shortly after the transfusion, the general decided to move the wounded to a safer place. I was part of the group that left. That night, the Germans gave a surprise attack on the town, where the others were still encamped. Lily was still recovering from giving her blood, and never made it out." Edith faltered, blinking back the tears. Her eyes rested upon the parents' faces. They were raw with emotion. "I never got to thank her."

The room was quiet for a moment, but heavy with emotion. The woman's husband wrapped his arm around her gently, trying somehow to console her. He breathed in deeply. "Edith, thank you for being a friend to our daughter. Our one comfort is that she is with the Lord now, and that she died bravely, in saving your life."

Edith twisted her hands, clenching them tightly. "I just wish she was still alive." She looked earnestly at them, brushing a hand across her face. "Please let me know if there is ever anything I can do for you."

"Thank you, Edith. We do appreciate it." The man's tone was low, but the gratitude in his voice was unmistakable.

"I don't want to take any more of your time." Edith stood up, and quietly left the room, not wanting to cause any more pain.

The streets were alive with people bustling around. A couple of soldiers walked towards her; one of the men possessed an armless sleeve, and the other bore the mark of a surgeon's knife across his face. They nodded politely to her as she passed them. It was a haunting reminder of War's permanent effects.

The soft hoot of a car horn interrupted her wandering thoughts. She scanned the street and then her gaze rested upon a black car parked against the curb.

Denni leaned out of the window, smiling cheerily at her. She hurried over, pausing a second while he opened the door.

"How did it go?" He asked as the engine rumbled to life, his tone soft and caring.

Edith smiled a little; her eyes blurring at the memory. "It was alright. They were fine with me; it's just—"she stopped.

"Go on," Denni gently coaxed, his free hand slipping gently in hers.

"It's just I can't help but feel awful that she died because of me."

"I know, but do you think she'd want you to live the rest of your life constantly regretting her bravery, though? She's in a far better place now - there's no sorrow or pain in Heaven." His tone was soft and caring.

"Thank you," she whispered. "It does make it easier knowing she shared the same faith."

§

Three months later, Denni and Edith sat together on the two-seater swing hanging from the porch, watching the sun dip below the red-streaked horizon.

He slipped his hand over hers; she smiled at him, her eyes sparkling with such beauty he couldn't compare.

"In three days," he whispered.

She nestled her head into his shoulder. "I can't wait."

Two figures walked towards them, hidden by the rays of light. One was slightly taller and carried a limp with each step. Edith squinted, trying to see who they were.

"I wonder who's coming here at this time," she remarked to Denni.

He nodded slowly. "Yes, indeed."

A rapid movement on the strangers' side caused Edith to

spring up from her resting place with unusual speed.

"What's the matter? Who is it?" Denni asked as she flew down the steps towards the approaching figures. She didn't answer.

"Edith!"

"Mya!"

The two friends clung to each other in joyful surprise.

"What are you doing here?" Edith asked, almost breathless.

"I was allowed to go home." Mya's smile reached to the tips of her ears.

"Oh Mya, it's so good to see you again." A slight cough caught her attention and she beheld Edmund standing there, watching the two with an almost awkward look. "Edmund, you're here?" Her tone was surprised but friendly.

"Yes, I never regained use of my arm, so I was sent home; with *her*." He nodded in Mya's direction. A sweet smile danced upon her face, and her eyes sparkled in the dimming light.

"Oh, we're all home now, and safe." She glanced at the two with marked curiosity.

A slight tap on her shoulder brought Denni back to memory. "Sorry, this is my fiancé, Denni Alber." She slipped her hand into his.

"Good to meet you, Denni. I've heard a lot about you from Edith," Mya remarked, as the two men shook hands.

Two brave soldiers, Edith thought.

"Mya," she hesitated, not quite sure how to word her question. "I hope you don't mind me asking, but," she gestured to both of them. "Has something happened?"

Mya looked up into Edmund's eyes and nodded slowly. "Well?"

He smiled in return. "Ah yes, about that; you will recall how Mya spent so many hours faithfully reading God's Word to me?"

Edith's eyebrows raised when she heard him say "God's Word" as if he was agreeing to the Bible.

"Well, do carry on, please?" she begged, trying to keep her composure.

"After the first day, I decided that I wanted to read it for myself...then as I poured over it, I began realizing my need for a Saviour. I kept thinking what if I died and that made me consider my life. I knew I needed to repent of my sins and put my trust wholly in Christ. After I did that, I started talking to Mya about everything—"

"Well, yes at first, but soon I could see that he understood a lot more of the Bible than me; he was reading it so much—so I was the one then asking questions," Mya interjected with a warm smile.

Edmund nodded slightly, "After that, we soon realised that God had brought us together. I know I'm still a young believer, but I feel God's hand in this matter. I asked her to marry me, and she said yes."

"Oh Edmund, I'm so pleased for you both. And Mya, well done for persevering; God has blessed your obedience and willingness to listen to Him instead of your own desires." She looked at the couple and smiled warmly. "I look forward to your wedding."

Mya laughed a little. "Edith," she said, her tone half stern, but her eyes twinkled. "It's your wedding first, and don't you say no to that. We didn't come out here just to get married first. And we do need to arrange some things with my parents first. They've given us their blessing, but we still need time."

Edith's cheeks glowed. "Ok...well, as a matter of fact"— she glanced at Denni who replied with a slight nod—"we're getting married in three days. And of course, you're invited. That is, if you can make it. We'd love to have you there."

"Oh Edith, I'm so happy for you; for both of you. Of course, we can make it." Her face was a painting of joy.

"Well, then: I guess that's settled," she replied. The wind moaned softly, releasing shuddering breaths upon the land. She could hear the distant cries of dying and wounded men - a memory re-lived through a single sound.

The sky was a dark canopy dotted by shining lights that sparkled so beautifully. Moonlight splashed across the ground, dancing with the shadows of swaying trees.

The four friends, brought together by something so horrific as War - and united by their trust, courage, and faith - stood silently, remembering the fight they had been struggling against, and the fallen heroes of yesterday.

Edith closed her eyes; once again seeing her past so clearly in her mind. *Pearl Harbour; the bodies lying there. Screams that haunted and never stopped echoing through your ears. Pleas from the hundreds of men trapped inside the crippled USS Arizona.*

"Edith, are you all right?" Denni gently stroked her shoulder, staring tenderly into her eyes. She nodded.

"Yes…it's just the memories."

"I don't think I'll ever be able to forget the things we saw out there," he spoke quietly, staring into the dark night.

Edmund and Mya nodded gravely.

"But at least we have each other," Edith put on a brave voice, despite the throbbing she felt in her heart.

"Yes," he replied, slipping his hand into her own.

CHAPTER THIRTY-TWO

The walkway was adorned with delicate white flowers and crimson red roses. An archway formed from twisted branches laden with cherry blossoms shadowed the path. Tall trees danced gracefully in the gentle breeze; their deep green leaves a beautiful contrast to the pale pathway stones.

White chairs sat on the soft grass, rows of five on either side of the path. Petals laced the ground beside the archway, mingling colours adding a gorgeous touch. Several guests strolled across the lawn, each dressed in fine apparel.

"Please, be seated," the pastor, a tall man with a kindly expression, urged the people towards the waiting seats.

Inside the house, Edith stood in front of a tall, antique mirror. Her auburn hair fell in ringlets around her shoulders; tiny white flowers adorning it. Her blue eyes sparkled, and to some, they almost glistened with drops of pure happiness. A white dress hung gracefully around her slight form; resting around the edge of her shoulders and then gathering at her waist. Where the skirt reached the ground, a long and delicate train followed behind.

Mya stood beside her, finishing the final touches. Her dress was the colour of gold-kissed roses; the shades of pink turning darker as they descended.

Edith's father poked his head around the door—"Are you ready?" he asked.

Since their arrival a week ago, her parents had spent a lot of time helping prepare for the wedding; it had been a precious finale to their time together as a family.

Her smile was almost enough of an answer. "Yes," she replied, her face shining with excitement.

He slipped his arm into hers and they walked towards the door, Mya taking the lead.

As they stepped outside, Edith could hear the cello notes floating softly on the sweet-smelling air. Her dress swished slightly as she went down the lane. One step round the bend, and she stood on the walkway.

Denni stood under the archway; one hand behind his back, and the other leaning on a walking stick that was trembling in his grasp. He was dressed in a dark blue suit with a white tie. His eyes watched her as she walked down the cobbled stone aisle. A smile took over his face.

She looked at him every step of the way.

He held out his hand and she took it willingly. Love and dedication were written in both their expressions.

The pastor talked a little, exhorting and encouraging the happy couple. As they listened to Scripture being read, Edith and Denni watched each other with pure commitment.

As he read through their vows, Edith felt a little surge of unspeakable joy.

"Do you, Denni Alber, take Edith Blately, to be your wedded wife?"

Denni glanced at her, love dancing in his eyes, and replied, "I do."

"And do you, Edith Blately, take Denni Alber, to be your wedded husband?"

She smiled up at him with such a tender expression only love could write. "Yes, I do."

As Denni slipped the ring over Edith's finger, he looked into her eyes and mouthed, "I love you."

She blushed.

"It gives me great joy, then, to pronounce you husband and wife," The pastor smiled at the young couple.

Denni and Edith waited patiently for his next words, holding each other's hands.

The pastor looked at Denni and said, "You may now kiss your bride."

And so he did.

Five years later.

A small child played on the grass, soaking in the heat. His head was covered in curly rings. On the porch, Edith and Denni sat on the swing, watching the young one with amused expressions. A pair of crutches lay on the deck.

"He looks just like you," she commented.

"You think so?" he replied, stroking her hair.

She paused for a second, tenderly looking at the child. "Yes," she whispered.

"It's been eight years since we met each other," he spoke in an almost dream-like manner. "I can still see the battlefields so clearly in my mind. I won't forget them."

She nestled in his shoulder. "Neither will I. I love you so much."

"And I you, my darling."

Denni Jr. looked up, rushed towards them, and flung his arms around the slightly rounded figure of his mother.

"How long now?" his baby voice sent flutters of joy through Edith's heart.

"Oh darling, not yet. Soon, but you still have to wait." She smiled down at the little child. His chubby face looked back up at her; big brown eyes staring longingly into hers'.

"Will I have a brother or sister?" He asked, his mouth slowly forming each word.

Denni and Edith glanced at each other with a slight smile. "We don't know yet...but we will soon," Denni answered, lifting up his little son and placing him gently upon the remnant of his knee.

"Dadda, what happ'en to your leg?"

"Do you really want to hear that story again?" he teased, ruffling the little boy's hair.

"Yes," the child replied, with an adorable lisp.

"Ok then…" he paused, slipping a war-aged hand into Edith's. "Hang on a sec; wait here. I want to show you something this time." He stood up awkwardly, placing the child on the swing. Gathering his crutches, he hobbled inside and soon returned. His hands held a soft white cloth.

"Den-Den, I'm going to show you something very special." He unwrapped the cloth, revealing a small medal. The sunlight glinted off the metal.

Small hands grabbed at its circular shape but were gently pushed away. "Do you know what this is?"

"No, tell me, please," the child pleaded.

"It's quite a long story," Denni replied as the little boy nestled down, waiting to hear the words. "Alright. It was in the year 1939. Germany was on a mission; to take over the world…"

Two hours later, the young couple sat rocking gently on the swing, watching as the sun dipped below the golden horizon. The little child lay nestled between the two, wandering somewhere far away in the world of sleep.

"And that is how we met," he whispered, wrapping his arm around her shoulders.

The End

ACKNOWLEDGEMENTS

It's been an exciting process writing and publishing my first book. Although this story is set during World War II, I have been careful to not include too many specific factual details as I wanted to use creative license. The characters in this book are fictitious but the setting is based upon true historical events.

Above all, I want to thank my Lord and Saviour, Jesus Christ, for His saving grace, and for the privilege of being able to write for His glory (1 Cor. 10:31)

I also want to thank my family who dedicated a tremendous amount of time to reading this book, editing it, and giving much-needed feedback and creative input. Your help was invaluable and I love you all so much!

Also, to my friends and beta readers who spent time giving feedback – thank you so much!

§

To find out more about my writing and stay updated with new releases, visit **abigailrebekah.com**.

www.ingramcontent.com/pod-product-compliance
Ingram Content Group UK Ltd.
Pitfield, Milton Keynes, MK11 3LW, UK
UKHW021843250325
456708UK00009B/97